From the videotaped last will and testament of Max McKendrick

Trace, as my oldest and most driven nephew, I aim to leave you my Silver Spur Ranch lumber operation, roughly a quarter million acres, which will give you the largest outfit in the West, bar none. But there's one hitch. You must marry Susannah Hart—again.

Since you two mavericks barely made it out of the chute before splitting up the first time around, I believe you owe yourselves a second chance. And if I were a betting man, which I am—well…*was*— I'd wager my fortune that you'd make a happy life together.

Besides, if you don't take the walk in forty-eight hours, you won't be inheriting your piece of my estate. And since I've fixed it so you and Susannah will be stuck together till kingdom come regardless, you might as well make the best of it!

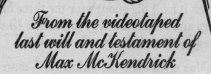

Dear Reader,

The Silver Spur Ranch has a quarter million acres,
but even it isn't big enough for the three McKendrick
siblings and the intended spouses their Uncle Max
has bequeathed them. No place really is!

Once Max gives them the ultimatum—marry the mate
he's chosen for them within 48 hours or lose their
inheritance—it's a virtual stampede!

Join Cathy Gillen Thacker as she brings you all the
sexy cowboys and wacky weddings you'd expect from
WILD WEST WEDDINGS!

Don't miss any of the three WILD WEST WEDDINGS
titles. The West was never like this!

Debra Matteucci
Senior Editor & Editorial Coordinator
Harlequin
300 E. 42nd St.
New York, NY 10017

Cathy Gillen Thacker

THE MAVERICK MARRIAGE

Harlequin Books

**TORONTO • NEW YORK • LONDON
AMSTERDAM • PARIS • SYDNEY • HAMBURG
STOCKHOLM • ATHENS • TOKYO • MILAN
MADRID • WARSAW • BUDAPEST • AUCKLAND**

ISBN 0-373-16633-8

THE MAVERICK MARRIAGE

Copyright © 1996 by Cathy Gillen Thacker

Chapter One

Susannah Hart turned away from the open cargo doors of her navy blue Suburban, her arms full of cookbooks, a hopelessly stubborn look on her pretty face. It was clear she had seen him coming, Trace McKendrick thought, as they had arrived at the Silver Spur Ranch logging camp at precisely the same time, and parked side by side in the camp-kitchen parking lot. Trace knew, even before the beautiful dark-haired, dark-eyed woman who had once been his bride lifted a dark, querying eyebrow, that she did not welcome his presence. But then, he thought grimly, that was no surprise. They had not exactly ended their short, unhappy marriage seventeen years ago on a pleasant note.

"What are you doing here?" Susannah demanded hotly as their eyes locked in that fiery way he remembered all too well.

Trace planted his legs firmly apart. Silently he pushed back the edges of his dark suit-coat and braced his hands on his waist. And then said, "I could ask the same of you."

"Your uncle Max told me that you were so busy with your own lumber company in the northern part of the state, that I didn't have to worry about running into you here, on his property.''

"Normally, that's true," Trace drawled.

"Because if I had thought there was even a remote chance I'd run into you again," Susannah continued, "I never would have accepted this consulting job."

Taken aback, Trace paused. He had assumed Susannah, who had reportedly been living in California ever since she had walked out on him, was back in Montana because she knew about the terms of his eccentric uncle Max's will. Obviously, that was not the case.

Curious about what else his uncle Max had been up to, besides matchmaking, he asked cautiously, "What consulting job?"

Susannah shifted the stack of cookbooks to her other arm and smoothed a strand of her short coffee-colored hair back into place. Her sable brown eyes still fastened on his as she replied, "Your uncle Max hired me to revamp the menus for the logging-camp kitchen so the same meal isn't served more than once a month. He also asked me to find a new head chef for the camp, since the old chef, Biscuits, quit on such short notice, which I have already done. Her name is Gillian Taylor and she starts tomorrow morning with the breakfast shift. I've already promised to be here to help her get acclimated. This evening, the food will be catered by Pearl's Diner, as it has been for the last couple of weeks. Now, if you don't mind, Trace," Susannah continued in a crisp, professional tone, "I have a lot of work to do."

Trace sighed inwardly as he speculated on what her reaction to his uncle Max's will was going to be. Ten to one, she wouldn't appreciate the gauntlet they were going to have to run to get to their inheritances any more than he did. Nevertheless, she had to be told. "We have to talk."

Susannah's slender spine stiffened militantly as she regarded him. "I can't imagine what about," she replied dryly.

Trace folded his arms in front of him. "You don't know?"

Susannah shut both cargo doors and swung back around to face him. "Know what?"

"About Uncle Max," Trace said quietly, wishing like hell he did not have to personally deliver the news to her. Unlike he and Susannah, Max and Susannah had always gotten along rather well.

Susannah blinked at Trace in obvious confusion. "What about Max? I just spoke to him a few days ago."

There was no other way to say it. "Max is dead, Susannah."

Without warning, Susannah's flawless golden skin lost it's sun-kissed glow. Her soft full lips trembled. "Dead," she echoed, clearly stunned. Tears glistened in her eyes as she laid a hand across her heart, as if that would somehow stem the hurt.

Trace swallowed around the knot of grief in his own throat and forced himself to continue gruffly with a recitation of the facts. "He died a couple of days ago. He had a heart attack in his attorney, Cisco Kidd's law office."

"Oh, no. Oh, Trace. I'm so sorry."

Her compassionate words were heartfelt. He was not sure why since so many of the expressions of sympathy he had heard the past few days had left him cold, but hers did him a world of good. "We all are," he concurred huskily.

"Max was a good man."

"Yes. He was." Trace fell silent.

"So why are you here?" she asked warily after a moment. Her eyes narrowed suspiciously, as she once again assumed the worst of him. "To tell me my services as consultant are no longer needed?"

Trace had to admit, had it been up to him, had he even known about it, he would not have hired Susannah to be anywhere near the Silver Spur Ranch. And not just because the renowned chef was pretty enough to cause riots in the all-male logging camp. At thirty-eight, her slender figure was as reed-slim as it had been at twenty-one, the curves on her five-foot-six-inch frame just as subtle and enticing. But there the similarities stopped. Where her thick and silky sable hair had once been long and flowing, it was now cut in the sleek chin-length bob that flattered the oval lines of her face. Her sable brown eyes were still wide and glimmering with intelligence, but there was a soul-deep wariness in them now—and a determination to hold him firmly at bay that had not been there before.

She was dressed in a short blue denim skirt, white T-shirt and matching blue denim vest. She wore trim white sneakers and crew socks on her feet that, while still plain in that suburban-mom way, also drew attention to the sensational sexiness of her legs.

Trace sighed. He had always loved her legs.

Hell. He had loved all of her, every sweet soft sexy inch...

"Well?" Clearly irritated with his brief perusal and lapse down memory lane, Susannah opened the Suburban's cargo door and set her cookbooks inside next to a laptop computer and compact portable printer. Propping her ringless left hand on her hip, she lifted her face to his. "What's it going to be, Trace? Am I out of here or not?"

He knew immediately what his answer was going to be. Wise or not, it didn't seem to matter. "I'm not going to fire you," Trace told her gruffly. *I just might haul you into my arms and kiss you just for the hell of it, if you keep glaring at me like that, though.* It would be interesting, he thought, to gauge her reaction. To see if she still melted in his arms the way she always had...

"What a relief."

"You expected me to, though?"

"That was the trouble with us, Trace. I never knew what to expect from you. Still don't," Susannah said as another car pulled into the lot. Trace recognized Cisco Kidd, his uncle's attorney. Dressed in his Western-cut suit, he looked every bit the successful Montana lawyer he had become, and nothing of the streetwise kid Max had rescued years ago off the mean streets of Butte, and patiently taken under his wing.

It had taken a while, but Cisco was now as much a part of Max McKendrick's "family" as the two nephews and niece he had raised. Trace wondered why Max had left nothing in his will for Cisco. Or had he? Trace decided that was something he needed to find out, when he had the time.

"Trace. Susannah." Cisco tipped his bone-colored Stetson in greeting. "I'm glad I caught up with you." As Cisco strode toward them, Trace noticed that the man had a portable television with built-in videocassette recorder in one hand, a black videocassette in the other.

"Max wanted you to have this." Cisco handed over both the television and the videocassette marked Last Will and Testament of Max McKendrick, Part IV, with the cautioning words, "It has pretty specific instructions in it. I think you and Susannah better watch it together."

Susannah turned to Trace in what had to be genuine astonishment. "I'm in Max's will?"

Trace nodded, already having witnessed some—but knowing Max, probably not all—of what was in store for them. "It's all explained on the tape."

"Then I'll be taking off," Cisco said with a wave. He opened his suit coat to reveal the cell phone he had stored in his pocket. "I'll be stopping by again later to make sure everything is going all right. In the meantime, call me if you need anything, Trace."

"Will do." Trace waved at Cisco as the attorney headed out once again.

"Why would you and I need anything from Cisco?" Susannah turned to Trace in amazement as the man drove off.

Trace sighed wearily. With a nod toward the logging-camp kitchen door, he placed his palm on the small of Susannah's back to steer her across the parking lot. "I think we had better go inside, watch the tape in private and let Max explain to us what he has in mind."

MOMENTS LATER, they hooked up the small television in the manager's office, behind the dining room. Trace and Susannah pulled up two wooden chairs. As soon as they were settled, Trace switched on the set and VCR and popped in the tape.

Within seconds, Uncle Max, clad in his trademark fringed buckskin jacket, mustard-yellow chaps and silver spurs, appeared on the screen. Though Trace knew his uncle had died within minutes of making his videotaped will, there was no sign on the tape of Max's impending departure from this world. His skin was a deep leathery tan beneath his long lone-star mustache, his white shoulder-length hair thick and shiny-clean. Nearly as old as the hills, the wildly successful Montana rancher and self-made man was still as energetic as the day was long.

On-screen, Max slapped his knee and began to speak. "Hello, Trace and Susannah. I reckon you two have had your first meeting by now, which—unless I miss my guess, considering the past—probably did not go too well. Not to worry. You two have plenty of time to iron things out between you before the wedding— forty-eight hours, as a matter of fact."

"Wait a minute. What wedding?" Susannah interrupted. "Who's getting married?"

"He's getting to that," Trace said.

"Knowing Trace, he hasn't explained much to you, Susannah. He's more than likely too busy taking charge of the situation and giving orders."

Susannah glared at Trace before turning back to the screen. "You're right as usual, Max," she murmured.

"But before I quit jawin' and cut to the chase," Max continued with the down-home directness for which he was known far and wide, "I've got something of a personal nature to say." Briefly, Max's ocean-blue eyes glimmered with sadness. "Trace, I think you know that for a long time now I've blamed myself for the demise of your brief marriage to Susannah. Many a time I've thought that if I hadn't given you that financial stake so you could start your own company right off and prove yourself to the world the way I knew you were just itching to do, you would not have ignored your young bride the way you did.

"And maybe—" Max frowned "—if I hadn't agreed to your mutual request to handle your quickie divorce for you, and instead had made you two young'uns wait and think about it, the way I'd made you think about getting married in the first place, the two of you would still be happily married to each other and bringing up a passel of kids."

"But we aren't married," Susannah protested passionately at the on-screen Max. "And we haven't been for some time."

"Amen to that," Trace muttered, glad Susannah was as upset as he was about Max's unexpected no-holds-barred examination of his and Susannah's romantic history.

"Now I know the two of you went on to get married to others and have two great kids each," Uncle Max continued affably. "Fate was no kinder to you there. Illness hit both families, and in the last five years, you both lost your spouses. And that sad twist of fate got me to thinking. Trace's two boys need a mama, and Susannah's two boys need a daddy."

"Oh, no," Susannah moaned, cradling her head in her hands as she apparently saw where this was going.

"My feelings exactly when I first heard about it," Trace muttered.

"So why not combine the two households and give your prematurely ended marriage another shot?" Max proposed cheerfully.

As if the two of them marrying again was the solution to everything, Trace fumed.

"So here's the deal," Max went on frankly, leaning in close and once again energetically slapping his buckskin-clad knee.

"Trace, I know how stubborn you are, and needless to say, that goes double when you've been hurt the way you were when Susannah walked out on you seventeen years ago. But you will never find a woman as fine as her if you look the whole world over. So it's time you gave the love of your life a ration of forgiveness and another chance to make you as happy as you deserve to be.

"And Susannah," Max said in a stern but loving voice, "the same goes for you. I know Trace was more absent than present the first time around, but you need to give him another shot at this marriage business and let him show you what kind of husband he could be to you when he is around.

"Which is why, I am leaving Susannah the hunting lodge in the woods, where the two of you lived when you were first married. As well as a chance to publish that series of cookbooks and instructional videotapes she's been a'wanting to make. Naturally, my publishing company, McKendrick Books for a Lifetime, will handle the deal, and by the time they are finished promoting and publishing your recipe collections, Susannah, you will be the Martha Stewart of the West."

"Oh, Max, that is so sweet of you, to help me get published," Susannah murmured, clearly pleased.

Unfortunately, Trace thought, not only was she willfully overlooking Max's suggestion that they rekindle their earlier romance and remarry, she hadn't heard half of what his eccentric uncle had in store for them. "There's more," Trace told Susannah grimly, having already heard part I of the will. And the second, more specific part of the will, he thought, Susannah was guaranteed *not* to like.

On-screen, Max continued seriously, "Trace, I am giving you the Silver Spur lumber operation and all the land it is situated on, which includes roughly one-third, or a quarter-million acres, of my Silver Spur Ranch. That, in conjunction with your own McKendrick Logging, Incorporated, will give you the largest lumber outfit in the West, bar none. I am also giving you the new state-of-the-art ranch house I built up on Silver Spur Lake. It is large enough to house both your boys and Susannah's, and the two of you, and I hope you will be very happy there."

Susannah lifted her eyes heavenward in what appeared to be a silent request for patience. "Now he's dreaming," she said.

"I couldn't agree more," Trace announced stiffly.

Max leaned in closer to the camera. His blue eyes held a warning glint as he advised, "Should you Trace refuse to marry Susannah, you will lose all rights to the land and the lumber operation, maintaining only the new state-of-the-art ranch house on Silver Spur Lake."

"That's not fair!" Susannah interjected, upset.

Trace squared his shoulders. "I couldn't agree more," he repeated. It was unfair. Unfortunately, that did not change anything. So the two of them would

have to play the hand they had been dealt, not the hand
they wanted ...

"Should you, Susannah, refuse to marry Trace,
there will be no cookbook and videotape deal with my
publishing company. Mind you, Susannah, I don't
think you will turn down this opportunity. I've done
some checking and I know you are every bit as ambi-
tious as Trace is these days, and that for some time now
you have been yearning to get out of the restaurant-
chef and consulting business and into creating cookbooks. I also know you've always had a soft spot for
the hunting lodge in the woods—"

"Which up until now was supposed to go to me,"
Trace interjected unhappily.

"—so that goes to you, too, even if you don't choose
to marry Trace again. I think you ought to have a place
on the Silver Spur for you and your boys that will be
yours and theirs in perpetuity. And in any case, Trace
will have a place here for his sons, too. Same deal.
Neither property can be sold, traded or otherwise for
the rest of your lives. And the fact that the two homes
are more or less adjacent to each other will make it
easier for your boys to socialize."

"He's assuming an awful lot," Susannah muttered,
sounding distressed.

"He always has," Trace agreed mildly, feeling no
more excited about the possibility of being neighbors.
It had taken him years to get Susannah out of his heart
and mind. And now to have her thrust at him again, so
unexpectedly. It was going to bring up a lot of memories, good and bad.

"Naturally, I put a few strings on these gifts of
mine," Max continued from the screen. "One, you two

must stick to each other like glue and stay under the same roof for the next forty-eight hours, with only three thirty-minute breaks apart. You break the rules, and the deal is off.

"Should you agree to the terms of my will, however, which will, I might add, insure the financial security of your four kids for the rest of their lives, too, which is something important to think about," Max said practically, "I will expect you to show up at the triple wedding ceremony on the bull's-eye property, forty-eight hours from now, and get married right alongside Cody and his new bride, and Patience and her groom. As I said previously, in part I of my last will and testament, I've taken care of all the details, including the guest list, so all you need to do is get yourselves there."

Max smiled warmly at them both from the screen. "Either way, the two of you will be stuck together, living and maybe even working side by side, as long as you adhere to the terms of the will and remain on this ranch. So you might as well make the best of it.

"And that being the case, I've got some advice for the two of you. There's no use crying over spilt milk, 'cause what's done is done, ain't no changing it. That means, Susannah, that you are going to have to forget about what kind of neglectful husband Trace was in the past, and start thinking about what kind of husband he could be, with a little loving guidance from you. And Trace, I know Susannah hurt you something fierce, walking out on you and your marriage after only three months, but there's no way she can go back in time and fix that, either. So all you can do—all anyone can do— is move on, the best way you know how." Max raised his palm in a silencing gesture. "I know picking up where the two of you left off might seem an impossible task at the outset." His blue glance turned serious as he continued, "It's going to be a lot of work bringing those two young families of yours together and blending them into one. But I am confident that you two mavericks can do it. All you gotta do is listen to your hearts. 'Cause if you do, you'll know what to do when the time comes." Max tipped his hat at them. "Adios," he said softly. "And remember, I love you." The screen went blank.

48:00 hours and counting . . .

THE ROOM VIBRATED with a poignant silence. "I can't believe he's gone," Susannah murmured after a moment, her eyes full of tears. "Watching him on the videotape . . . Oh, Trace, he seemed so full of life."

"I know," Trace said thickly.

She wiped her eyes with a tissue. "Not that I agree with the terms of his will are in any way laudable—"

"None of us do," Trace lamented tightly.

Susannah got up to pitch her tissue into the trash. Turning back to him in a drift of her trademark White Linen perfume, she asked curiously, "What was all that about Patience and Cody?"

Trace stood and restlessly prowled the tiny linoleum-floored office. "Patience never got over being jilted at the altar. She's been wanting to have a baby, via artificial insemination." He leaned against the file cabinet, crossing his arms in front of him. "Max was opposed to her going to a clinic and having a stranger father her child . . ."

Susannah leaned against the opposite corner, next to the chalkboard that traditionally carried the menus for the week. "I can imagine he would be."

Trace nodded in agreement, continuing, "So Max left Patience the horse-breeding operation and hired a ranch veterinarian, Josh Colter, to help her run it. Unfortunately, to Patience's chagrin, Max also wants Josh to marry Patience and sire her children."

Susannah's eyebrows drew together in a perplexed frown. "Did Patience know this man, or something?"

"No. In fact, she had never even met him. That's what makes it all the crazier, but you know how eccentric my uncle could be when he sets his mind on making something happen. No path is too far out of the way."

"Tell me about it," Susannah murmured empathetically.

"Not that her situation is any better than Cody's," Trace continued candidly, glad to focus on someone else's problems rather than his own.

Looking almost afraid to inquire, Susannah said, "What did Max arrange for Cody?"

Trace paused, not sure where to start with that one. In some ways, Cody was fast becoming as unpredictably eccentric and frontier-wild as Max had been. While Patience was as free with advice to the lovelorn that she never seemed to follow herself. And he was passionately interested in building a business empire.

Aware Susannah was still waiting for him to tell all, Trace sighed and rubbed the tense muscles in the back of his neck. "Have you seen Cody lately?"

"Not since he was a kid," Susannah said with an eloquent shrug.

"Well, he eloped with Callie Sheridan to Mexico seven years ago. Apparently, Callie ran out on him during their honeymoon, before their marriage was ever consummated. Cody's been something of a...well, a wildman, ever since. Hasn't shaved or cut his hair or wanted anything to do with another woman, period. Thinking Cody was never going to marry, Max found a bride for him, through this Western Ranch Wives video-matchmaking service. Cody's none too happy about marrying a woman he has never even laid eyes on, of course, but in deference to Max's last wishes, he at least went off to meet her."

Susannah shook her head, looking absolutely flabbergasted. Which was, Trace thought, the way all three of them had felt when part I of the will was played for them earlier, at the Fort Benton Gentlemen's Club.

"Poor Cody," Susannah murmured compassionately. "Patience, too."

Trace studied her, unable to help but notice the direction her sympathy was aimed. He quirked an inquiring eyebrow, then drawled, "But not, I gather, poor us?"

"I didn't say that!" Susannah retorted, flushing with embarrassment. It was impossible to believe after all these years apart that Trace could still read as accurately between the lines as ever, at least where she was concerned.

Like it or not, there was a part of her that was glad to see him, just as there was a part of her that was terrified. If he ever found out the real reason she had left him years ago, there would be hell to pay, she knew it.

But there was no way he was going to find that out, she reassured herself. Not if she were cool and collected. And so completely, unexpectedly, outwardly greedy that she threw him off the track.

"Well, I'm willing," she announced breezily, with a willingness to do absolutely anything for money that she certainly did not feel. "How about you?"

"You'll marry me again? Just like that?"

Susannah shrugged, wishing the small room didn't feel so cramped. It wasn't as if she didn't know the man. The two of them were intimately acquainted with each other in every way. So what if he was a seasoned, mature, capable-of-anything thirty-eight now, instead of a gung-ho, fresh-out-of-college twenty-one? So what if he had the impeccable dress, short-cropped hair and take-charge manner of the wildly successful CEO that he was? He still had the same broad shoulders and solidly muscled, rugged, logger's build on his imposing six-foot-two-inch frame, the same classically handsome features, stubborn and somewhat angular jaw and probing ocean blue eyes. Heck, he even probably kissed and made love the same. So it wasn't as if she had anything to be afraid of. Did she?

"It's not as if we haven't done it before," Susannah said a lot more cavalierly than she felt. Only this time, she thought wisely, they could have their brief marriage in name only.

"It's not as if we haven't done anything before," Trace replied as he crossed the small room in two long strides, and in a move that seemed as much testing as it was territorial, put both his hands lightly on her waist.

Susannah planted her palm on his chest and backed out of his staying grip to keep him at bay. "I did not say *that* was part of the deal," she said firmly.

He regarded her in silence. After a moment, he said quietly, "You really want the cookbook deal, don't you?"

Actually, Susannah thought wearily, what she wanted was to be able to support her family in the style to which they had become accustomed, provide for their college educations, and be able to spend more time with her two boys. No easy task for a single mom.

Figuring it would do no harm to admit as much, she told Trace frankly, "The last few years have left us all feeling pretty burned-out on big-city life. And I'm not just talking about the horrendous traffic or the high cost of living or the increasing crime in Los Angeles. We've also had to deal with the fires caused by the Santa Ana winds, which swept incredibly close to our home. Then there were the mud slides and floods from the torrential rains. Before that, the riots. The upshot is, I've been wanting to get my boys out of the city and into a safer, more tranquil environment for some time now. And those feelings multiplied tenfold after the last quake."

Trace looked upset. "You weren't hurt?" he asked quickly.

"No." Susannah shook her head. "None of us were home at the time, thank God. But our house was damaged structurally and declared a total loss. Except for the personal affects we were able to salvage—we lost everything." And that for her had been the last straw.

"Insurance?"

"Our policy didn't cover earthquake damage. To get one that did was too expensive. And though the government was offering low-cost loans for rebuilding, I wasn't sure I wanted to do that, either, I wasn't sure my nerves could take it. So I moved us into temporary housing, and put our lot on the market, hoping to sell.''

''No takers.''

''None. Of course, being that close to a major fault line, I expected as much.'' Susannah released a heart-felt sigh as she thought back to the turmoil and hardship of the past year. ''Anyway, it was not long after that when I first came in contact with Max. He appeared on the scene, with an offer to bring me and my boys to the Silver Spur and consult, with the possibility of a permanent position in one of several of the restaurants he owns in Helena. I had no idea he knew about my desire to publish my own series of cookbooks, though.''

''When was this?'' Trace questioned.

''A couple of months ago. I told him I couldn't come until the boys finished the school year. He was most gracious about the delay, even later when Biscuits unexpectedly quit as head chef in the camp kitchen.'' Susannah tilted her head back and searched his face. ''You're sure Max didn't mention any of this to you?''

''No. Not a word. Not even in part I of the will.'' Trace narrowed his blue eyes at her thoroughly. ''But you knew we'd meet up?''

Susannah drew a deep, steadying breath. ''Actually, I was counting on just the opposite happening, since Max had told me you and your two boys were living in northern Montana, near McKendrick Logging, Inc. Knowing what a workaholic you are…'' She shrugged her shoulders. ''I just didn't imagine you'd get all the way down here while I was consulting.'' She could see now what a mistake in judgment that had been.

Trace frowned. "Well, that makes two of us." He ran a hand through his elegantly cropped wheat blond hair. "I didn't expect to see you, either."

Susannah couldn't help it; she had to ask. "Sorry you did?"

Trace kept his eyes on hers. "I don't know," he said slowly, his steady gaze never wavering. "It's brought back a lot of memories."

How well she knew that. "None of them pleasant?" Susannah guessed.

"There's nothing warm and fuzzy about having your bride of three months announce she's leaving you because you came home late the night before."

"It wasn't just one night that you didn't arrive home until midnight, Trace. It was practically every night. When I saw that wasn't going to change, when I realized I couldn't live like that, I had to leave. But you—" Susannah shook her head in disbelief "—you *still* act surprised by the sheer inevitability of it all." Surely by now he had figured out how much he had hurt her, by putting all his time and energy into his work and none into their marriage!

Trace backed up to the desk and sat down on the edge of it. "It's not as if you gave me any clues you were unhappy, before your coolly worded announcement that last night," he retorted calmly.

He was being deliberately dense, and she did not appreciate it. "I was not going to let you turn me into a nagging shrew," she told him, turning and erasing the several-weeks-old menus from the chalkboard on the wall. "If you didn't want to be home in the evenings or on weekends, even when I asked you to be home for a special romantic dinner for two...then that was just the way it was." She put down the eraser with a thud. "I knew I couldn't change it. I couldn't change you." Nor had she been sure she was right to try. "The bottom line was, you gave me no choice, Trace. I had to leave."

"You did have a choice, Susannah. You could have tried to stay and work out our problems. As for your unhappiness," he continued, a muscle working in his jaw, "I know I was gone a lot, but I was working hard to build a home for us."

Susannah had not let him get away with that notion then, and she was not going to let him get away with it now, no matter how reassuring it was to him, in retrospect. "Correction," she retorted, vaguely aware that her voice was rising. "You were working hard to build a career for you."

Trace rolled lithely to his feet. "For both of us," he stressed.

"Whatever." Susannah backed up until her back touched the blackboard. "The bottom line is that we're together less than half an hour and we're already bickering about our different wants and needs."

Trace was silent.

"And though that may be the reality of the situation, I doubt that's what Max had in mind," Susannah continued, aware she felt like crying again, for a completely different reason.

"No doubt Max believed we would have a fairy-tale ending this time around." Trace scowled as he jerked loose the knot in his tie.

"Yes, well," Susannah said, feeling depressed. "We know better now, don't we?" she continued with a weariness that came straight from her soul.

Trace unbuttoned the top of his heavily starched white shirt, exposing the strong suntanned column of his throat. He studied her in silence, his gaze moving over her hair, face, lips, before returning once again to probe her eyes. "So, are you willing to help me gain my inheritance?" he asked point-blank, following his question with a searing look.

"You want what he's offered, don't you?" Susannah asked, knowing he did. His ambition to be successful in the business world was clearly as all-consuming as ever.

Trace shrugged, not too shy to admit his desire as he took off his suit coat and tossed it on the desk. "As Max pointed out on his videotape, if I combine our two holdings, I'll have the largest lumber company in the West. Hell, yes, I want it," he confirmed adamantly, rolling up his sleeves.

His glance lowered to hers. "Do you?"

I didn't ask for this, Susannah thought, but as long as Fate tossed the opportunity my way.... Telling herself she needed to be driven by practicality and not emotion, she replied, "I need a new home. I need to get myself and the boys out of California and away from any more earthquakes, fires, floods, riots, and whatever else L.A. might decide to throw our way before the decade ends. And yes, I want that cookbook deal. Because if I get that, I can start working out of my home, and I'll have more time to spend with my sons."

Trace edged closer, a satisfied smile on his handsome face. "So, we're in agreement then?" he said softly.

"It would appear so, yes."

"Forty-eight hours."

Susannah thought of her boys and focused firmly on the future. "I think we can handle it, if we set our hearts and minds to it." She and her boys stood to benefit so much, as did Trace and his children. And after all, it was only forty-eight hours they were talking about here, she reassured herself sagely. Not a lifetime. Enough time to forgive each other, as Max wanted, and then move on, as she and Trace wanted...

Trace quirked an eyebrow. "I don't know about hearts, but I've a mind to make it work," he told her firmly, his dedication to doing just that steadfast. "The only question is, what are we going to tell our kids?"

Chapter Two

"The truth," Susannah said.

Trace's eyes lasered on hers, held. "That we're honoring Max's last wishes—"

She nodded, completing his sentence the way she had when they were married. "As a way of honoring his memory, nothing more."

"So we'll share quarters and stick to each other like glue for the next forty-eight hours, just like Max wanted," Trace confirmed.

"We marry, then inherit, and divorce as soon as the terms of the will and propriety permit." Deciding they were standing much too close, Susannah stepped past Trace and moved toward the door of the tiny office.

Following her lead, Trace picked up his suit coat and slung it over his shoulder. He looked very sexy with his tie loosened, shirt collar undone, the beginnings of a five-o'clock shadow lining his handsome face. "You think they'll buy it?" he asked as he fell into step beside her, as naturally as if they had never been apart.

Susannah let her gaze rove the short, mussed layers of his hair. "If they understand how much we both loved and respected Max, yes, I think they will."

Susannah's heart raced as they walked out into the adjacent dining hall. She told herself it was the stress of seeing him so unexpectedly, and in such intimate circumstances, that had her feeling so completely aware of him, so on edge. In an effort to regain her composure, she looked around. Long wooden trestle tables were bordered by benches on each side. A cafeteria-style buffet was set up next to the kitchen, at the far end of the room. According to her notes, the camp fed three hundred men daily. It would be a challenge creating diverse menus that would please nearly everyone.

"How much more do you have to do here?" Trace asked as they threaded their way through the tables.

"I'm finished," Susannah said, taking a last look around before she stepped outside and locked up, while he held the screen door open for her. Finished, she stepped back, so they were no longer in such proximity and tilted her head to look at Trace. "I have to be here first thing tomorrow morning, though. I promised Pearl I would help out with the breakfast shift, and that's also when Gillian Taylor, the new head cook, is due to arrive." She shrugged apologetically as she deposited the key to the camp kitchen and dining hall in her purse.

Susannah walked as far as their four-wheel-drive vehicles, then stopped. "Unfortunately, because we have to stick together like glue, that means you will have to get up at the crack of dawn and come with me."

"No problem. I'm an early riser and I have plenty of work to do on my laptop, so I'll come with you."

Susannah breathed a sigh of relief. Unable to help herself, she shook her head and murmured softly, "It's working out fine already."

His glance moved over her languidly, taking her in from head to toe and all places in between. "You seem surprised," he noted casually.

Her body warming wherever his eyes had scanned, Susannah focused instead on the towering woods that stretched as far as the eye could see. "As you should be, considering we were about as easily mixed as water and oil."

"It seems a long time ago."

"Yes. It does. Doesn't it?" Susannah fell silent. She had forgotten how beautiful the woods were, and how lonely.

"Where are your boys now?" Trace asked, bringing her out of her reverie.

Susannah tensed slightly, aware they were headed into dangerous territory. Territory she hadn't expected to have to cover with him. "Scott, my oldest, is participating in the Summer Scholar program at the University of Texas in Austin so he won't be joining us, but Mickey, my youngest, is here with me. He was taking a tour of the logging camp with one of the loggers who was kind enough to volunteer to show him around. Mickey's something of an adventurer, he always wants to see and do everything. They should be back any—" She glanced at her watch, then looked in the direction of the gravel road behind the cabins that housed the loggers who chose to live on the property, at least during the work week, and grinned. "There they are now." She lifted her hand in a wave, motioning them over.

Susannah's eight-year-old son Mickey, a rambunctious-looking, freckled-face boy with light brown hair and a grin, raced toward them. As always, his shirttail was half in, half out. He had dirt smudged on both knees. His sneakers were covered with mud. No matter how Susannah tried, no matter how she admonished him, she simply could not keep her son neat and clean for more than a few minutes at a time. Smiling at him as he neared them, she wondered if that would ever change...

"Mom, Mom, it was so cool!" Mickey skidded breathlessly to a halt in front of them.

Susannah put her hands on Mickey's shoulders and brought him in close to her side. She was glad to see him, but there were important things to be done before she and Mickey exchanged notes on their afternoon. "Whoa, now. First things first." She looked down at Mickey and said gently, "Did you thank Mr. Turner for showing you around?"

"Thanks." Mickey beamed at Tom Turner, a bearded, burly, fifty-something logger in a flannel shirt, jeans and heavy work-boots, and continued to enthuse, "I had fun. I mean it. The woods are way cool. And I 'specially liked that river we looked at, with all the churnin' white water, and those big gray rocks!"

"You're a good kid." Tom Turner swept off his yellow hard hat in deference to Susannah's presence, then reached over to ruffle Mickey's hair. "Come back in about ten years or so, and I'll give you a summer job, you hear?" After extracting Mickey's promise that he would indeed do that, Tom looked at Trace. His expression sobered abruptly. "I heard about Max," he said softly, holding his hat flat against his chest.

"We're all sorry and thinking of you and the family. We're gonna miss him."

"We all will," Trace said.

Tom nodded, his grief as evident as his worry over the future. "We also expect there'll be some changes around here?"

"A few. Not too many," Trace told him. "I'll be over first thing tomorrow morning to discuss them with you."

"I'll look forward to it," Tom replied. "See you later, Susannah."

"Thanks again, Tom."

Mickey looked from Susannah to Trace and back again, his curiosity evident.

"Mickey, this is Trace McKendrick. He and I were married a long time ago, before I met your dad."

"But you're still friends?" Mickey asked, cutting right to the heart of the matter, as usual.

Were they? Susannah wondered. To her surprise, it was beginning to feel as if they might be. "Yes, I guess we sort of are, though we haven't seen each other for a very long time. It's a long story, and I'll fill you in on all the details later, but we are going to forget about the hotel and stay with Trace and his two boys for a few days, in their new ranch house."

"Cool," Mickey said, using his favorite word yet again. Bubbling energy, he glanced at Trace. "How old are your kids?"

"Fourteen and ten," Trace answered with the kind of smile that told Susannah he genuinely liked kids. "How old are you?"

"Eight."

"That's a pretty fun age," Trace retorted with a paternal kindness that made Susannah's heart ache.

"Yep." Mickey grinned proudly. "I'm old enough to do all sorts of neat things now. Like go to work with my mom sometimes. And bus tables and everything."

Trace's grin widened even more. "I bet you're a big help."

"Yep," Mickey said, his expression abruptly dead serious. "I really am."

"Speaking of sons, where are yours right now, Trace?" Susannah asked curiously.

"I left them at the ranch house. That was about four hours ago. I think I better get a move on and check on them."

"One car or two?" Susannah asked, not sure she wanted to be that close to him for any length of time. Already, she was far too aware of the invigoratingly male scent of his after-shave, the appealing sun-kissed glow of his hair and skin, the easy warmth of his touch.

But it seemed there was no helping it as Trace paused and mentally reviewed the stipulations attached to his uncle's will, just as she was doing.

"I think we better go in one car, as per Max's wishes," he said after a moment. "Don't you?"

FORTUNATELY Mickey chattered incessantly the whole way back to the lakeside ranch house, about everything he had seen and done at logging-crew boss Tom Turner's side. From time to time, Trace answered some of Mickey's questions about the vast rolling forests on the Silver Spur, leaving Susannah to admire the majesty of her surroundings.

She had forgotten just how beautiful the Silver Spur was in June. She and Trace had first met and fallen in love in June, and married the following September. It seemed so long ago, and yet it seemed like yesterday, she thought as she looked around and saw that the endless emerald green forests were interrupted only by glimpses of the meandering Silver River and small meadows dotted with wildflowers. The granite rise of the mountains loomed on the horizon. In the distance, the mirrorlike surface of Silver Lake gleamed a stunning dark blue between the stands of pine, birch and aspen. In front of that was a huge three-story log-cabin–style ranch house. It had a broad front porch, with a porch swing on each end, and half a dozen rocking chairs scattered about. Hanging baskets of brightly colored geraniums, and a well-landscaped yard, complete with a variety of shrubs and flowers, added to the welcoming warmth of the sprawling ranch house.

"Oh, Trace," Susannah breathed as he parked his Jeep in the driveway, and they all got out. She looked at the numerous windows and the steep slate roof. "It's gorgeous."

Trace nodded, his pride in the new home Max had left him evident. "Max went all out when he built this place," he confirmed.

Susannah looked around the well-manicured front lawn. The lake behind them was small, private, and this was the only house on it. Yet she thought she recognized the rocky slopes on the opposite side of the glistening lake. "We used to picnic up here, didn't we?"

Trace nodded. "On this very site."

So he remembered, too. She turned toward him and tipping her head to him, asked softly so only he could hear, "Part of Max's plan to reunite us?"

He nodded. His expression thoughtful, he kept his eyes locked on hers. "No doubt."

Mickey was already headed toward a soccer goal and ball in the side yard. He turned back to Trace. "Would anybody mind if I kick around the ball a little?"

Trace smiled. "Go right ahead."

Not quite ready to go in yet, to face the fact that they were going to be living together under the same roof for the next forty-eight hours, Susannah put a staying hand on his arm. As for the bedroom arrangements—the possibility that she might be seeing Trace the last thing before she went to bed at night and the first thing in the morning—she didn't even want to think about that. She swallowed, forced herself to put her own worries aside. They had others to consider here, too. "How do you think your boys are going to take this?" she asked.

Trace shrugged, looking as if there was absolutely nothing in this world he could not handle. "There's only one way to find out," he predicted with an encouraging half smile just as the front door opened. Two boys came out. The first was a bespectacled teenager, with dark brown, short straight hair, who looked a lot like Trace must've looked at that age, except slightly more studious, Susannah thought. He was carrying a thick computer manual and a sheaf of printouts beneath his arm. "Hey, Dad, I think I solved that accounting problem you were having," he said.

"Great going, Nate," Trace said, patting his son's shoulder in congratulations. He knew the boys had been broken up about their uncle's sudden death, but they had vented their grief and were handling it well, the way Max would have wanted them to. "I can't wait to hear all about it as soon as we have time to sit down a minute."

The second boy was Trace's ten-year-old Susannah decided. He, too, had medium-brown hair, worn slightly longer than his older brother's, with a cowlick at the back that looked absolutely untamable. Dressed in tennis shoes, a wild Hawaiian-print shirt and baggy khakis, he had his hands shoved deep in his pockets and a mischievous look on his face. He high-fived Trace and drawled, "Hey, Dad, what's happening?"

"As a matter of fact, Jason," Trace began, "quite a lot. Susannah, here, and I have a lot to—"

Before he could finish his sentence, the sound of a car engine in the driveway had them all turning once again. In unison, they watched as Cisco Kidd pulled in and parked his car right behind Trace's Jeep Wagoneer. Susannah felt her heart stop when she saw who was in the passenger seat.

"LOOK WHO I found hitchhiking on the road," Cisco announced, clearly not understanding, Susannah thought, the import of what he had just done, bringing her older son to Trace's door. Nevertheless, she plunged on, making introductions. "Trace, this is my son Scott. Scott, this is Trace McKendrick."

His manner polite but distracted, Scott said hello to Trace and shook his hand before turning back to Susannah. He gave her a sly grin. "Before you start, Mom, let me just say how glad I am to be here," he began with disarming affability.

As usual, he was dressed in jeans and a T-shirt. To-day's sported the University of Texas logo on the front and Ten Reasons Why Friends Don't Let Friends Go To Texas A&M on the back. His wheat-blond hair was straight, windblown and on the longish side, which meant he hadn't got that haircut Susannah had told him to get, once he arrived in Austin, either.

Susannah wasn't interested in any smooth talk. Scott was supposed to be in Texas! Not Montana. And what had he been doing hitchhiking, for heaven's sake. He damn well knew better than that! "What are you do-ing here?" she demanded pointedly of her son, look-ing straight into his guileless blue eyes.

Scott rubbed his chin, where a handful of whiskers were growing. It seemed he had forgotten to shave, too, in the week he had been at the month-long camp. "Well, uh, that's a little tricky, Mom," Scott said ca-sually.

Susannah folded her arms in front of her. "I am all ears."

Scott tossed his duffel down in front of him. "I got kicked out of camp."

Susannah had feared as much. Scott hadn't wanted to go in the first place. She had just been so desperate to keep him out of Montana, until she finished her business at the Silver Spur Ranch and got settled else-where, far away from Trace and Max and all the rest of the McKendricks. "And no one told me?" Susannah asked her son incredulously.

"Hey!" Scott palmed his chest emphatically. "They didn't even tell *me* yet!"

"Back up and start from the beginning," Trace interjected. Unlike Susannah, he looked mildly amused by her son's antics and very interested in the details.

"Okay." Scott drew a deep breath. "You know how they had all those camps going at UT at once?"

Susannah sighed, almost sure she was going to wish she didn't know all the details when her son finally finished his tale of woe. Not about to shirk her duty as a responsible parent, however, she continued prodding him, "I'm listening."

Scott flushed. Whether with delight or embarrassment, Susannah could not tell. "Well, I uh, sort of organized a—" Scott paused and narrowed his eyes at Susannah. "You sure you want me to tell you?"

"No," Susannah admitted readily as she gave her son yet another quelling look. "But I have a feeling I need to know, anyway."

Scott shrugged and, shoving his hands into the back pockets of his jeans, launched back into his story. "The guys in the Summer Scholar program decided to pay a visit to the girls in the UT Tennis Camp, which just happened to be housed on the floor above us. It wasn't easy getting by the chaperons stationed at the elevators and the stairwells, but . . . well, never mind about that. Anyway, some of the, uh, girls, um, let's say unmentionables just happened to get, uh, confiscated during this—"

"In my day, I believe it was called a panty raid," Cisco interjected dryly.

"Uh, yeah." Scott shrugged and reveled in the envious glances of the other kids, and the stunned glances of the adults. "Anyway, they were looking for the ringleader of the commando raid on the girls and somehow my name got bandied about.''

"Were you the ringleader?'' Susannah asked, already fearing she knew the answer to that.

In answer, Scott flashed a youthful grimace. "I think I'll take the Fifth on that." He paused to look away for a second before daring to look back at his mother. "Anyway,'' he continued, as if it were the most logical thing in the world, "I got wind of the fact they were getting ready to kick me out and send me home, as an example to everyone else, so I just packed my bags and lit out, saved them the trouble of having them call me in and give me a lecture, you know.''

Susannah could imagine. Since the last earthquake, though he wasn't in it, Scott had adopted a devil-may-care demeanor that seemed to get him and his friends in trouble more often than not. She was worried about him. She knew she had to find a way to turn him around. "So, no one at the camp knows where you are,'' she ascertained calmly, knowing nothing would be gained by her losing her temper with her son. Though she had to admit she was sorely tempted to do just that.

"For all I know, they aren't even aware I'm really missing yet.''

Susannah turned to Cisco. She knew she needed to calm down and get a few more details before she spoke to the camp director. "Would you mind calling the camp and letting them know that Scott is here with me and that I'll be in touch with them as soon as I can?''

"No problem. Trace, okay if I go in and use your phone?'' Cisco asked.

"Go right ahead.''

Susannah turned to Trace. She ran her hands through her hair, pushing it off her face, tucking the ends of her bob behind her ears. "I think I need a moment to collect myself. Maybe talk to Scott here—"

"Hey, if it's going to be another one of those 'you're going to be sixteen in a few days or weeks or whatever,'" Scott interrupted unhappily.

At the mention of her son's age, Trace went very still.

Susannah swallowed. It took every bit of self-control she possessed to tear her eyes from Trace's and turn to her son. *No, not now, please,* she thought, her heart pounding. "Scott," she reprimanded.

Trace stepped between Susannah and Scott. "When is your birthday?" Trace asked Scott softly.

Thinking he was about to be rescued from further scolding, Scott reported with a cheeky grin, "In two weeks, three days and about six and a half hours. Not that I'm counting every second until I can get my driver's license, you understand," he joked.

Susannah slowly let out the breath she had been holding. "I think you should understand your driver's license is tied to good behavior," Susannah retorted, hoping Trace wasn't thinking what she feared he was. But it was too late. She could see by the shell-shocked look on his face and the sudden tensing of his broad shoulders that Trace had already done the math.

Cisco came out of the house. "All taken care of."

Somehow, Susannah forced a smile. "Thanks."

"I'll see you all later." The attorney was off with a wave.

"'Bye, Cisco," everyone said more or less in unison.

Trace waited tranquilly until Cisco had driven off then looked at Susannah. She noted that beneath her former husband's surface elation, there was a ruddy hint of color across his cheekbones, a cool gleam in his blue eyes. Which could only mean one thing, she thought nervously. Trace was already assessing the situation, devising a plan that would allow him to come out on top.

Her confidence at being able to handle this, handle him, dropped another notch.

He gave her a smile that did not reach his eyes. "May I speak to you a moment?" he said politely.

"Not now," Susannah said. *I need time to think about how I am going to explain this in a way that you don't hate me forever or land us both in court.*

"Yes, now," Trace stated softly.

"The kids," Susannah protested.

Trace had that figured out, too. "Boys, Susannah and I have to check on the hunting lodge," he announced.

"Cool!" Jason enthused as he broke into an energetic bout of shadow-boxing. "I love it out there. Can we go, too?"

"Not today," Trace decreed autocratically and immediately earned frowns from all four of the boys. "Maybe tomorrow," he promised. "While we're gone, Mickey and Scott can settle in and unpack. Nate and Jason, you show them to their rooms."

"Who should sleep where?" Nate asked with a perplexed frown. "After all, there are six bedrooms and—"

"You all figure it out," Trace said in the decisive tone of a general handing out orders to his troops. He grabbed Susannah's arm beneath the elbow and steered her in the direction of his dark green Jeep.

She went, for the same reason she allowed his orders to stand uncontested: she didn't want a scene in front of the boys. Efficient seconds later, she and Trace were backing out of the driveway. Her throat dry, her heart slamming against her ribs, she cast a look over her shoulder and saw the boys had lined up, brothers against brothers, in the front yard. To her unease, they didn't look particularly thrilled to be forced to keep company with one another. She bit her lip uncertainly. It wasn't enough that Trace was ticked off at her. They had another battle brewing, too. "I'm not so sure it was a good idea leaving them all alone so soon. Goodness, Trace, they don't even know one another."

Trace brushed off her worry with a dismissive shake of his head. "They'll be fine."

You don't know Scott and his recent all-out propensity for mischief, she thought. Not that Trace's youngest son, Jason, looked like a stranger to shenanigans, either.

Trace slanted her a warning look as he continued humorlessly, "It's you and I you should be worried about, Susannah. Unless I miss my guess," he said heavily, his blue eyes glittering with a combination of anger and remorse, "you have some explaining to do."

TRACE PARKED the Jeep in the gravel lane in front of the hunting lodge. As Susannah looked at the building, she was assaulted by bittersweet memories. Trace, carrying her over the threshold the night they returned from their brief honeymoon, then making wonderful passionate love to her all evening long. Trace, forgetting to show up for dinner, night after lonely night. The two of them never touching, hardly ever even speaking.... She couldn't go back to that, she just couldn't.

She turned to him. Judging from the unerringly grim look on his face, he was thinking the same thing. She swallowed around the knot of emotion gathering in her throat and tried to still the sudden trembling of her heart. "I don't think it was such a good idea, coming here."

"I think it's the perfect place." Trace pushed from the Jeep. Now that they were alone, he looked as if he wanted to explode. "After all, our child was conceived here, wasn't he, Susannah?"

Susannah sucked in a steadying breath and joined him on the gravel lane. She had always feared this day would come. Now that it was here, she didn't quite know how to handle it. And apparently, neither did Trace.

Abruptly, Trace looked as though he wanted to hit something with his fist. "I notice you're not denying it," he said brusquely, towering over her.

Susannah shrugged and tried not to notice how his broad shoulders blocked out the light of the sun. "It's clear you've already put two and two together."

Another silence. He gave her a slow once-over. "Why didn't you tell me?"

She laughed shakily as tears filled her eyes. He made it all sound so easy, and it hadn't been. "I tried."

"No," he corrected grimly, a muscle working convulsively in his cheek as he kept his eyes steadfastly on hers. "You didn't."

Susannah took a step back, and then another and another. She stood with her hands folded beneath her breasts, her legs braced slightly apart, the gravel beneath her feet digging into the soles of her white sneakers. "Don't you remember the night before I left you for good?" she reminded him hotly, working hard to keep her own skyrocketing emotions under wraps. "I said I had something important to tell you. I asked you to come home for dinner by 8:00 p.m., like I had every night for the three months before that. You said you would and then I waited for you. And I waited. And waited. You finally showed up around 2:00 a.m. You were sorry, as always. Another problem at the office, you said. Undaunted, I *still* tried to tell you, but you said you were too tired to talk, could it wait until morning, and then you hit the sack and went to sleep the moment your head hit the pillow."

Trace flushed with guilt. "I admit I was insensitive that last night we were together," he said.

"And then some."

"And maybe not the best husband in the world for the first couple months we were married."

"You're damn straight about that," Susannah retorted harshly.

"But couldn't you have just blurted it out?"

Yes, Susannah thought. She could have. But she had wanted it to be a memorable occasion, something wonderful to hold on to in the years ahead. Unhappily, her plans had turned out to be as futile as their marriage had been.

"Why? What would have been the point?" she stormed back with an indignant toss of her head. She aimed an accusing finger at his chest. "I know what a responsible person you are. I know you would have done the right thing, at least fiscally, and insist I stay.

It wouldn't have made us any happier. At that point, you didn't know what to do with a wife, never mind a baby.'' Tears flooded her eyes once again. ''Scott would have been just one other person who was in the way of you achieving your dream of building your own lumber company.'' And she hadn't been able to bear the thought of seeing her baby hurt the way she had been.

''So the next morning you packed your things, told me our marriage was a mistake from the get-go, and you wanted out,'' Trace surmised, his hurt at the memory of their last emotion-charged conversation evident.

Susannah tried like hell not to let his pain get to her. After all, she had given him every chance to come after her and make things right between them and he hadn't. Not that day or any other. ''You made your feelings for me, or maybe I should say lack of them, pretty clear when you immediately agreed to my request for a no-fault divorce.''

His expression impassive, he took another step nearer. ''I knew you were right, that I hadn't begun to make you happy.'' He shrugged emotionlessly. ''That being the case, I didn't feel I had the right to stand in your way, if a divorce was what you wanted.''

No, Trace, Susannah thought with a weariness that came straight from her soul. *What I wanted back then was you, and our child, and a life together.*

''Our feelings for each other aside...'' He took her by the shoulders and held her in front of him implacably. ''You still should have told me,'' he reiterated in a low voice laced with anguish. ''Dammit, I had a right to share in such wonderful news. I had a right to know I was going to be a father!''

Susannah stared straight at the suntanned column of his throat and the open collar of his shirt. As she realized the validity of his argument, she was swamped with feelings of guilt and remorse. And most of all, loss. "You're right. As a mature adult, I agree, I should have told you that I was pregnant before I left you. At the very least, I should have telephoned or written you when Scott was born." She paused, her lower lip quivering slightly.

Trace's hands tightened possessively on her shoulders. "Then why didn't you?" he demanded hoarsely, still struggling to understand. And perhaps, forgive.

Susannah turned her back and walked away from him. Pain tightened every muscle in her body. "Because it was years before I came to that realization," she said, facing him again. "And by then I was already married to a man who did want a child, even if it wasn't his. In all the ways that count, Scott knew Drew as his father. I couldn't break that up," she said quietly, unable to hide the depth and breadth of her regret that she hadn't acted with more foresight seventeen years ago. "Had I done so at that point, it would have been devastating to everyone."

Trace did not disagree with her on that; neither did he sympathize. "Did my uncle Max know about Scott?" he asked point-blank.

Susannah stared at the light dusting of dark wheat-gold hair on Trace's arms. "I don't know. He knew about my wanting to write cookbooks. He knew enough to realize that the last quake in Northridge was enough to make me want to leave California for good.

He got me out here on a consulting job and wrote me into his will. What do you think?'' She lifted her face to his. "Did he know, or at least guess?''

Trace shrugged his broad shoulders and went back to lean against the front bumper of his Jeep. His mood introspective, he put a foot on the bumper, and rested his forearm on his bent knee. "He might have known. He could do math, too." The silence stretched between them interminably.

"Which is why, I suppose," Trace continued after a moment, "you insisted Scott go to camp in Texas while you were here, so I wouldn't run across him, if I happened to visit the Silver Spur Ranch."

Ignoring the quiet accusation in Trace's deep blue eyes, Susannah lifted her chin. "Scott has been going to a summer camp of some sort or other every year since he was ten, and it was a good experience for him. At least it would have been, if he hadn't been kicked out."

Trace took a moment to absorb that as some of the hurt left his eyes. Abruptly, he was all-business once again. "Does Scott misbehave often?" he asked, quickly shifting into his problem-solving mode.

Susannah went back to lean against the bumper, too. Like Trace, she had no desire to go inside the hunting lodge that had also served as their home when they were newlyweds. She studied the toe of her sneaker with more than necessary care. "The last quake, even though he wasn't in it, put Scott on a life-is-too-short-not-to-have-fun kick. I'm hoping it's just a phase, but right now. . . . I don't know. I have to turn him around. That's one reason I was thinking of moving back to Montana," she confided candidly, wanting Trace to know that he had not seen Scott at his best, but rather his worst.

"The bottom line being that given a choice, you weren't going to tell me, even now, about my son," Trace concluded grimly, aware it was taking every bit of self-control he had to keep his own tumultuous feelings in check.

Discovering he and Susannah had a son . . . a son he had never met until today had hit like a sucker punch to the gut. The fact that Scott was obviously well-loved and well-cared for did nothing to dull or negate his anger and disappointment in Susannah. Added to his fury was his hurt. The numbing knowledge of all the years he had missed. The times with his son that could never—would never—be regained. How did one get over something like this? he wondered. How could he? When right now all he wanted to do was balance the scales and make some of the betrayal and sharp disappointment he felt go away.

"What good would it have done to tell you that now?" she countered rhetorically, moving away from the bumper. Her voice faltered abruptly. For a moment, she couldn't go on. "It was water over the dam and—"

"You're wrong about that, Susannah," Trace said, his gaze resting on her face as he cocked a faintly mocking eyebrow in her direction.

Susannah's skin paled at the deliberateness of his low tone. She seemed to know as well as he that he was not about to just let this go. "What do you mean?" she demanded, beginning to panic.

His expression as sternly indomitable as his mood, Trace grabbed her hand and tugged her back to his

side. "Max has given us the perfect opportunity to
right a mighty big injustice," he said as he swiftly saw
a way to get back that which had been stolen from him.
He clamped an arm around her waist and hauled her
close. Sliding a hand beneath her chin, he tilted her face
to his. "And whether you like it or not, I plan for us to
do just that."

Chapter Three

Trembling, Susannah flattened her hands across his chest, effectively wedging distance between them. "Listen to me, Trace. I am not—I repeat, not—giving him up!"

Trace shifted, so her back was to his Jeep. "I didn't ask you to give him up. I am asking you to share him with me, Susannah."

Susannah's eyes widened incredulously as her emotions ran riot. This was exactly what she had been afraid of all along, exactly what had kept her from telling Trace about his son sooner. "We can't tell Scott you're his father!"

"But I could be his stepfather." Trace gave her just enough time to let the information sink in, then continued in a hard tone that brooked no dissension. "We're going to get married, Susannah, just like Max wanted. Only we're going to stay married and live together in the same house after the ceremony, too."

Susannah couldn't seem to get any oxygen into her lungs. "You're crazy," she panted. Not only that, he was asking the impossible!

"Try determined," Trace corrected, tightening his grasp on her waist. "You robbed me of the first sixteen years of my son's life, you are not robbing me of what is left. Nor do I want to take him away from you," he added.

Her heart thudding heavily in her chest, Susannah stared up at him with trepidation. "And if I disagree?" she questioned, stunned she could sound so calm when she felt as if her entire world, and that of her eldest son's, was falling apart.

Trace shrugged and continued to look as unmovable as a five-ton boulder. "One way or another, he is living with me. It's up to you whether or not you want to be there, too." Apparently satisfied that he had gotten his message across, he slowly released her.

Susannah stumbled backward until she was leaning up against the front of his Jeep, the sun-warmed metal pressed against her skin. Feeling as though she were in a bad dream from which she could not awake, she studied him for long, tense moments. "You'd really force me into marriage."

He kept his eyes on hers as his lips curled sardonically. "I never believed it until this moment," he countered, regarding her with cool satisfaction now that he had taken complete charge of the situation—and them—again, "but revenge *is* sweet."

Susannah studied the woods behind the stone-and-timber hunting lodge until she had regained her equilibrium and felt ready to face him again. Swinging back to Trace—who was at that moment rebuttoning his shirt and reknotting his tie—she looked directly into his eyes and advised him calmly, "If you think we're going to fool the boys, you're sadly mistaken. They'll know when we're not sleeping together that something is up. And then they'll be determined to find out what."

"Oh, but we are going to be sleeping together," Trace announced with a supreme male confidence that grated on her nerves, as he rolled down his shirtsleeves and rebuttoned the cuffs.

"Like hell we are," Susannah retorted.

"How else are we going to enact an air of normalcy?" Trace grabbed his suit jacket out of the back of the Jeep, and slipped it on. "Besides, sex was never a problem with us, Susannah."

She watched him slip into the CEO role again, the role in which he was most comfortable. "You're right. Communication was our problem. And once again, you're not listening to me. I am not signing on to be your bartered slave."

He quirked an eyebrow in her direction. "I believe it's called a wife."

"Whatever you want to call it, I am not doing it!" Susannah stormed.

"Then get a damn good lawyer, 'cause I'll see you in court." Still straightening the lapels of his suit coat, he headed for the driver's side.

Seeing a disaster in the making, Susannah hurried after him. "Trace. Wait—"

He whirled on her. "I *have been* waiting, for sixteen-some years now. I want my chance to be a father to the son I never knew I had." He glowered at her, then pushed on after a meditative pause. "If you want to be his mother, too, then you know what you have to do."

Susannah studied Trace's ferocious scowl and knew what path to take. "All right. I'll marry you," she decided, swiftly following his lead and seeing a way to manage him, and their situation, too. "And I'll stay married to you," she finished determinedly. "But only on one condition."

"And that is?" he prodded her uneasily.

"No sex. Not now. Not ever."

TRACE STUDIED SUSANNAH, hardly able to believe how much his life had changed in the hour since she had been tossed back into his life. One moment he had been the grieving father of two and the CEO of his own company. Now, he was still grieving the loss of Max—he sensed he would be for some time—but he was the father of three, not two, about to become a husband again and stepfather to yet a fourth child.

Worse, Max had set up the will so he and Susannah would be neighbors—at least in terms of property owned—for the rest of their natural-born lives.

Initially, of course, he had thought he could handle that arrangement. In fact, he had been determined to take charge of the situation and turn it to his advantage, the same way he did every other tricky situation he came across in the business world. And then move on.

Now he couldn't do that. Staying angry with Susannah would be a waste of time and energy, and he did not waste either. Hence, he would have to forgive her. They would have to work together to handle the boys. Maybe he would never be able to love or trust her again in the no-holds-barred way he once had, but eventually they would become close again, on some level. And when that happened, Trace thought... "You really think we can live together in the same house, night and day, and not eventually end up in bed together?"

"Why not? It worked before," she said tartly, reminding Trace of all the dinners and evenings together he had missed by working so hard. "Besides, it always comes back to the same thing," Susannah continued with a sort of resigned affability. "We have our four boys to think about. An example to set. What kind of example would we be setting if we embark on a licentious affair right under their noses?"

"It wouldn't be an affair," Trace told her. "We'd be married."

"Not where it counts, not in our hearts." Silence fell between them. Susannah went to sit on the steps of the hunting lodge. She clasped her hands together and, leaning forward, locked them around her knees. "Look, I am the first to admit I made a mistake," she told Trace passionately. "But how was I to know back then that you would ever even want to be a father, never mind an apparently very good one?"

Glad she was so willing to work things out, even if it was only out of a need to assuage her deep-seated guilt, Trace went over and sat beside her. Like her, he was in no rush to revisit the inside of the home where they had spent the early tumultuous days of their ill-fated marriage. "How do you know what kind of father I am?" he asked curiously.

Susannah gave him a smile of pure maternal bliss. "I just met your boys, remember?" she said softly. "They were happy, well-cared for. The love and respect and admiration they felt for you was obvious just by the way they looked at you and spoke to you."

Trace turned toward her slightly. Their thighs bumped in the process. Determined to keep his mind on the truce they were working out, instead of how soft she felt or how good she smelled, he forced himself to forget how sexy she looked with her windswept hair, soft bare mouth and dark sable eyes.

He lifted a skeptical eyebrow. "You could tell all that in one five-minute exchange?"

"I'm a parent," she said firmly. "I know what I see."

"For the record, you seem like a very good mother, too," Trace admitted grudgingly.

"Thank you."

"That being the case, once we work out the minor problems in combining our two households into one, we'd make a good team."

A GOOD TEAM?

There he went, making business deals again with the aplomb of a master, Susannah fumed, taking exception to his annoyingly matter-of-fact attitude. And that's all this was, she thought sadly, a business deal. He found a problem, turned it into a challenge to be conquered and then arrived at a way to come out on top. It was the summons to excel that mattered to him, and nothing else. Not her. Maybe not even Scott, though she doubted he realized that, yet.

Unable to sit still a moment longer, she vaulted to her feet. Deciding to look around a bit, she slid her hands into the pockets of her denim skirt and took the path that wound its way around to the back of the lodge, Trace following her languorously.

"A good marriage is impossible without true love, Trace," she told him as she ducked a hanging vine. She had learned that the hard way. Without it, people were just roommates, or friends, not husband and wife, not as husband and wife should be.

"Then call it a marriage on the outside and think of it as a most practical arrangement on the inside," Trace suggested.

Still stinging from his practical-to-a-fault attitude, Susannah stepped past several rosebushes badly in need of pruning and moved onto the flagstone patio. She thought about the time she and Trace had dragged out a pile of blankets and made love there, under the stars. It had been one of the few nights he had made it home before midnight.

She sighed, her spirits plummeting once again, as she headed off the raised patio, and down the path to the old-fashioned wishing well. "It doesn't matter what we call it, or how we think of it, my boys will never buy our suddenly deciding to get and stay married, no matter what the terms of Max's will. My sons know me better than that. They know I'd never just get married for convenience. And if my boys doubt it, yours soon will, too," she predicted sagely.

Trace watched as she cranked up the bucket, tested the cool water with her fingertips, dumped it out, then sent it back down again. "Then we'll have to give them a reason they can accept besides the will," he said.

Her eyebrows arching, she gave him a questioning look. "That reason being?" she said as she brought up the bucket again, brimming with fresh water.

"Chemistry, pure and simple," he said, watching as Susannah lifted the dipper to her lips and drank until her thirst was quenched.

Having had her fill of the pure springwater, she handed him the dipper. "Dream on."

He took a long thirsty drink. "You're the one who's dreaming if you think that chemistry like ours ever fades or goes away."

Susannah turned her back on him again. She would not let herself be seduced by the memory of the night on the patio all those years ago, or the few days of happiness they'd had together on their honeymoon, before he settled into his work.

"Well, it does," she said quietly.

Trace sent the bucket down to the bottom of the well. "Not in our case, it hasn't." He moved to stand beside her, so they were both looking at the sun as it descended in the western sky.

"What does that have to do with our getting married?" Susannah started back, around the rest of the lodge. Even if they didn't go inside, she was determined to finish exploring the perimeter.

Trace caught her around the waist and drew her against him. "We'll prove to all four of our boys that the chemistry we once felt still exists between us, and that it's strong enough to make us fall madly in love with each other again."

Susannah blew out a disgruntled laugh as she brushed the windswept hair from her face with the tips of her fingers. She could only imagine how he planned to do that. Already her heart was pounding and she had a peculiar weakness in her knees. She felt flustered, even as she was seduced by the warmth and strength and smell of him. "They'll never buy that, Trace," she murmured, hoping like heck she was putting on a rousing good show of indifference. Her eyes lifted to his as she dared him to try to prove otherwise. "I don't even buy it."

He threaded his hands in her hair and tilted her face to his with movements that were both slow and excruciatingly sensual. His glance roved her lips, watching as they parted in an O of surprise. "Then I'll just have to convince you, won't I?" he murmured.

One touch of his lips to hers and she was half out of her mind with wanting him. Swept up in memories, in a longing so deep and fierce it was a physical ache. With a murmur of surprise that the passion did still exist after all this time, Susannah found herself moving unconsciously closer in his embrace. And as their bodies melded together, and his hands swept down her back then up to her breasts, leaving ribbons of fire in their wake, she found herself surrendering, just a tiny bit.

Enough to open her lips to the insistent pressure of his. Enough to want to taste and touch and kiss him back, as deeply and passionately and possessively as he was kissing her.

She wanted him. She wanted him more than she ever had in her life. But she did not want to be kissed just to prove a point. She did not want him making love to her as a means to an end—in this case, their son.

Knowing that if she didn't end the fiery embrace soon, she wouldn't end it at all, she tore her mouth from the compelling pressure of his, and wrenched herself out of his arms. She took another deep, oxygen-starved breath to steady herself. "You're out of line, Trace."

"Am I, Susannah?" Trace gave her a level look that let her know, for all his outward acceptance and businesslike affability, and despite his efforts to put her deception quickly behind them, deep inside, where it really counted, he was still steaming at her for robbing him of his firstborn child, and would be for some time. "Then we're even," he said quietly, letting her know in a glance that through the marriage of convenience, he really intended to make her pay for what she'd done. "And it still doesn't change a thing."

HE SHOULDN'T HAVE kissed her that way. Trace knew it, now that the kiss had come to an abrupt halt, and he had known it before the kiss even started. And maybe he had kissed her out of a need for revenge, or to punish her. But he had been unable to resist showing her, in the most potent, devastating way possible, exactly what she had robbed them of when she'd run out on him like that. Taking not just their son, but all they could have—would have—shared if only they'd stayed married. If only she had stayed to work things out....

"You're not going to give up, are you?" she said.

Trace shrugged and figured he might as well be honest. After all, she wasn't the only one who had been hurt. "Let's just say I found out today how wrong I was to let you walk out on our commitment to each other seventeen years ago. So, no, I am not going to let you go again, not without a fight, not considering what is at stake."

Susannah drew a deep breath as he waited for her reply.

Could it work? Was she crazy to even be considering such a proposition?

She had no home: the last quake in Northridge had seen to that. She did not have sufficient insurance money to enable her to rebuild. Nor, considering the trauma of the recent fires, floods, riot and quakes, did she want to go back to Los Angeles. Montana was the only other home she had ever had. She had left because of Trace. It was ironic that Trace was the reason she would ultimately come back to her native state. And yet, it was oddly fitting, too.

Finally, she shook her head. "I don't know why I'm even listening to you," she confessed.

"Because you have no choice. Because you know I'm right. It's painfully obvious that Scott needs an enhanced sense of security right now. A mother and a father both could give him that. And Nate, Jason and Mickey could benefit from having two parents again, too." He paused for a moment, then said, "We were friends once. I'm not saying it's going to be easy, considering everything that has happened, but if we really work at it, if we view this as a challenge we can't walk away from, we could be friends again."

Susannah was silent as she headed back toward his Jeep. She had enough of their trip down memory lane. Besides, it was suppertime, and the boys would be wondering what had happened to them.

"What are you thinking?" Trace asked as he opened the passenger door for her.

That it would be nice to finally get rid of this mantle of guilt and remorse and fear I have been carrying all these years. She had done that in finally owning up to the truth with him.

Knowing this had to be said, if they were ever going to be friends again, never mind companionable husband and wife, Susannah delayed stepping into the Jeep. She regarded him honestly. "I'm sorry you had to find out the way you did."

"But not sorry I know?"

How could she be, when it felt as if a weight had been lifted off her shoulders? "Maybe it's better this way," she said after a moment, leaning back against the side of the Jeep. "Maybe we need to start dealing with the truth, while still going the whole nine yards to protect our kids from being hurt."

Trace's hand clenched around the top of the open Jeep door. "God knows it was what Max wanted." His glance roved her upturned face as his voice dropped another rueful notch. "He never stopped thinking you were the only woman for me, and vice versa."

Funny, Susannah thought, she had felt the same way for what seemed forever. She'd thought she was fooling herself, building up the romance of the past and the sheer physical passion she and Trace had shared into some hopelessly romantic fantasy of what could have been.

The sensational reality of his kiss had swiftly disabused her of that idea. If anything, her memories were on the tame side, when compared to the sizzling reality of being held in his arms. No one had ever been able to make her feel the way he did, so completely caught up in the physical side of love, and that was still true. As yearning swept through her yet again, she sighed softly.

Would it be so bad sharing quarters with him once more? Finding a way to be friends, to forgive each other, to make love not war? To jointly finish raising their son and the rest of their children and then move on with their lives, and in the process give all four boys both a mother and a father and a warm, loving home. In another ten years, even eight-year-old Mickey would be off to college. Susannah knew how fast time went. It had been seventeen years ago, she had married Trace, sixteen years and nine months since she had left him, and yet in many ways, it seemed like yesterday.

It wouldn't be like when they were first married, when she was alone all day, in that hunting lodge deep in the woods, waiting for her husband to come home to her. These days, she would have all four boys to keep her busy, and her work. The series of cookbooks would take years to write. And besides, if Trace still worked the long hours he had, he would hardly ever be home.

"Well, what's it going to be?" Trace said.

Susannah hesitated. She wanted to do what was right and fair. She also wanted to come through this with her heart intact. "You promise me you'll do everything in your power to make this work, if I agree?"

Trace nodded. "For the boys, yes."

Not for us, Susannah thought, a little startled by the sharpness of the disappointment that swept through her. But still, she bolstered her sagging spirits with an inner resoluteness that more than matched his, Trace's newfound attitude of cooperation was a start. She had expected him to be furious with her much longer.

"All right," she said finally, hoping like heck she was not making a mistake. "Because I owe you, because I truly want to make this up to you, we'll go into this with every intention of making it work in every way, not just for a couple of days or weeks, but long-term. But that is all I can promise you at this point, Trace. Good intentions. And my willingness to take it one day, one hour, one moment at a time." She paused, studying his face. It was impossible to tell what he was thinking about her stipulations. His expression was impassive. "Well, what do you think? Will this do?"

Trace shrugged and offered a satisfied half smile that lit up his deep blue eyes. "It'll have to, won't it?"

TEN MINUTES LATER, they were back at the lake and headed up the driveway. "When we tell the boys what's going on, let me do the talking," Trace told her in a low, intimate tone.

Susannah rolled her eyes, letting him know this was not the start she'd had in mind. "I know how much you enjoy being in charge of your own destiny and being the CEO of your own company, but you do not have to take charge of everything, Trace," Susannah told him dryly.

He quirked a dissenting eyebrow. "In my house, I do."

This they were going to have to work on, the sooner the better, Susannah thought passionately. "It will soon be *our* house, and in our house, we will both have an equal say," Susannah said mildly. She gave him a look that let him know right off the bat that she did not plan to negotiate on that, no matter how much he protested.

Trace sighed. And as she had hoped, eventually, gave in. "Agreed—reluctantly. For the sake of the kids."

"Whatever," Susannah retorted, just glad she had made one tiny inroad with him. Where Trace was concerned, it was going to be an uphill battle all the way.

Trace parked directly in front of the house. To Susannah's chagrin, the scene was quite different from when Trace's boys had been there alone. Then, in the late-afternoon sunshine, all had been peaceful and serene. Now, at sunset, with her boys on the premises, music was blaring from the open windows at rock-concert decibels, which was par for the course. But as for the rest... "That's strange," Susannah murmured, perplexed.

"What?"

"The front door is wide open. It's almost dark. Yet I don't see any lights on." Susannah shot an anxious look at Trace. She couldn't imagine the boys sitting around listening to music at top volume with the lights off. In fact, she couldn't imagine the boys *sitting,* period. "You don't think something has happened, do you?"

Abruptly, Trace looked a little worried, too. "There's one way to find out." He cut the engine on the Jeep and stepped out.

Susannah got out, too, and they headed toward the house. Trace stopped and frowned at the garden hose lying on the ground. It had been left turned on and, as they stood over it, water poured out of it in a steady stream. Seeing that, the hair on the back of Susannah's neck stood on end. Her heart pounding, she pointed at the hose. "Is this usual?" she asked anxiously.

"Not around here." Trace went to shut off the hose. "Your place?"

She slanted him a worried glance. "No. Never." Her boys knew better than to waste water.

Before she could say so, however, the air reverber-
ated loudly with the sound of metal clanging against
metal. The sounds of something heavy falling. Footsteps thudding across concrete. Everything seemed to
be happening at once, and everything seemed to be
coming from the rear of the ranch house.

"Wait here." Trace said firmly. He headed around
back.

"But—"

As take-charge as ever, he put out a hand, emphatically signaling her not to follow him.

Susannah was content to let him explore the back
alone. But she wasn't about to leave the boys in danger, when the front of the house still needed exploring. Holding her shoulder bag in one fist, like the
potential lethal weapon it was, she started stealthily
toward the front door.

Being careful to stay in the shadows, she peeked
around the open portal. What she saw really set her
heart pounding. To her right was a living room. Throw
pillows were tossed here and there. A lamp was overturned. To her left was a formal dining room. Several
ladder-back chairs were turned over on their sides. A
pool of some sort of liquid was streaming from beneath one of the chairs.

Stomach clenching, she started farther into the
darkened house, the loud music assaulting her ears.
She had just reached the kitchen, when Trace came at
her from the other side. He frowned as he saw she was
inside the house. He shouted to be heard over the
blaring music, "Have you seen the boys yet?"

Susannah shook her head as her stomach turned end
over end again. The kitchen was a wreck, too. Chairs

overturned, as well as a couple of soda cans. Chips, cookies, two half-eaten apples and more water, or maybe it was soda, were scattered everywhere.

Trace shot an apprehensive look at the front staircase. He was clearly as baffled as she. "I don't know what's happening here, but we better look on the second floor," he announced grimly.

Susannah gripped the banister hard and gulped as Trace started up the stairs, swiftly taking the lead. And she was still gripping it when an ear-splitting, absolutely inhuman war whoop sounded directly behind her head. Whirling halfway up the stairs, she raised her handbag in self-defense and stared into the soot-blackened face of an attacker, then ducked as the missile he aimed at her powered straight toward her head.

Chapter Four

Susannah screamed in surprise. More rampaging warriors appeared out of nowhere, and everyone shouted at once.

"Oh no!"

"It's Mom!"

"Not here!"

"Watch out!"

"Duck!"

Susannah did duck, as it happened, but not soon enough. *Splat,* a water balloon smashed against her thigh. *Smack,* one hit her in the shoulder. *Whack,* another hit her midchest. A fourth landed on her head.

Silence reigned for approximately one second. Still holding tightly to the banister, Susannah slowly straightened as water streamed down her face, shoulders, back, chest and legs. Trace walked back down toward her as her four attackers gathered round. All four were dressed in dark clothing. All four had smeared something—black grease or maybe the soot from the inside of the fireplace—on their faces. It would have been funny, if they hadn't made such a mess with their antics and she hadn't been so darn soaked.

Ten-year-old Jason shook his head in disgust. "Wrong person, you dork-face!"

"No kidding, Sherlock," Sixteen-year-old Scott drawled.

"Ha!" Eight-year-old Mickey crowed triumphantly. "You guys're in trouble now."

"Like you aren't?" Fourteen-year-old Nate asked, rolling his eyes in exasperation.

"Nate's right," Susannah confirmed autocratically. "You all had water balloons. You are all in trouble now. I don't care who started it," she continued, anticipating the next argument about to be launched.

"I'll second that." Trace had reached Susannah. Though the expression he aimed at the four boys was disapprovingly grim, he curved a gentle hand on her shoulder. "You okay?"

Besides the fact that she was cold and wet and her skin was still stinging from where she'd been hit, Susannah nodded, knowing she was glad he was there to face this chaos with her. "Sure." Together, Susannah and Trace descended the stairs. The boys parted to make way.

Trace went through the downstairs, switching on lights as he went. "Nate. Please get Susannah a couple of towels."

"Yes, sir." Nate dashed up the stairs and returned seconds later with two fluffy towels. Susannah wrapped one around her shoulders, for warmth. While Trace motioned for the boys to sit in the dining room chairs, she used the other to blot at her hair, face, arms and legs. Together, still standing, they faced their four sons.

"What has gotten into you boys?" Trace demanded quietly of Nate and Jason. "I've never known you to act like this."

"Scott and Mickey, although this is not the first time you've gotten into a water-balloon fight, you know better than to carry one inside the house," Susannah said sternly.

All four boys sighed audibly and shot one another loathing glances. "Well, we're still waiting for an explanation," Trace said when no reply was forthcoming.

Suddenly, everyone pointed at once. It was clearly brothers against brothers. "They started it!" all four clamored in unison.

"It doesn't matter who started it," Susannah reprimanded. "The point is, you've made quite a mess here," Susannah continued as it became clear this had not been good-natured fooling around, but all-out war. "I expect you to be on your very best behavior in the future, or I'm going to want to know why."

"That goes for you, too, Nate and Jason," Trace said. "And since Susannah and her boys are going to be staying with us for the new few days—"

"Whoa. When did this happen?" Nate interjected.

"A while ago. It seems Uncle Max left Susannah something in his will, too. But to collect it, she has to stay with us for the next two days. So, naturally her boys will be here with her, too."

"But you guys are divorced, aren't you?" Nate said.

Not for long, Susannah thought as she continued to blot some of the dampness from her hair and face.

"Yes, Susannah and I are divorced," Trace said seriously. "Although it seems now that Uncle Max never accepted that, because he has asked us to get married again, in forty-eight hours."

The jaws of all four boys dropped. "You're not going to do it, are you?" Scott gasped.

Trace frowned as he admitted, "We have no choice, if we want to collect our inheritances."

"And," Susannah added softly, locking her eyes with those of her eldest son, "we feel we should do our best to honor Max's wishes, since he was always very good to us both, and this was what he wanted."

"So, in other words, you're using each other to get what you want," Nate blurted out, pushing his glasses higher on the bridge of his nose.

"Does this include sex?" eight-year-old Mickey wanted to know as he rubbed at a big smudge of dirt on his knee.

"Of course not!" Jason interjected, sounding incensed, as he ineffectually smoothed his cowlick with the back of his hand. "They're too old to have sex!"

Sixteen-year-old Scott just shook his head and gave Trace and Susannah a smug what-am-I-going-to-do-with-you-two-kids grin. "I wouldn't bet on it," Scott drawled, looking like whatever happened, he did not want to be around to witness it. "In fact, now that I think of it, your dad and our mom are just at that funky midlife-crisis age where parents sometimes do all kinds of reckless irresponsible things."

"I assure you, Scott, Trace and I are not in the middle of a midlife crisis," Susannah interrupted, blushing fiercely despite herself. Although, considering what

Trace now knew, it felt like a crisis of a completely different kind.

"Furthermore, Susannah and I will not be sharing a bedroom," Trace said.

Because he doesn't want me or because he can't forgive me? Susannah wondered, recalling that their physical passion was the one thing, the only thing, the two of them had ever been able to completely depend upon in their relationship.

"How come?" Nate asked, a look of intellectual curiosity on his face.

"Because this marriage is one of friendship," Trace said.

Susannah didn't know if she was relieved or not about the sleeping arrangements, as dictated by Trace. She did know she resented Trace's controlling attitude. He couldn't keep himself from taking over, as if he were the only parent on the premises.

Now that they had the attention of the group, Trace continued, "Look, guys, combining two families under one roof—even temporarily—requires a team effort. So far, you boys aren't doing your share when it comes to getting along, but that can easily be fixed if you follow through on your responsibilities to us and to one another. So, what do you say?" Trace said, his look telling them it was more order than request, no matter how politely or genially worded. "How about helping us out here?"

In the face of Trace's insistence, all four boys mumbled a reluctant acquiescence.

Deciding to take advantage of the lull, Susannah turned back to the kids. "I think we had better get started cleaning up this mess, don't you?"

"The boys made the mess, not you or I," Trace interrupted. "They can repair the damage. I'll supervise." Hand on her shoulder, he pointed her toward the stairs. "In the meantime, you can go up, put on some dry clothes and relax."

"IT'S GOING to take them at least half an hour, if they work furiously," Trace reported minutes later, showing Susannah to her room on the second floor. He set down her suitcases inside the bedroom. "But I promised them no dinner until it's done, and they're all starving, so they should finish quickly."

Trying not to shiver, for the combination of wet clothes and cool evening air had left her feeling chilled to the bone, Susannah said, "I'll get something started then—"

Trace shook his head. "Nate is mopping the kitchen floor, as we speak."

He watched her take the warmest clothes she had brought with her—jeans and a sweatshirt—out of her suitcase. "Why don't you relax for a few minutes instead?" he suggested.

Susannah was acutely aware of the way Trace was leaning against the bureau, watching her every move. She added socks, a lacy bra and matching panties to the pile of clothes. She picked up the travel case containing her toiletries, and held it in front of her like a shield. "That's a little hard to do, don't you think?" she retorted, unable to completely suppress a shiver. "When you keep taking over, like you and you alone run the place and everyone in it?"

"You'll have your chance to be the parent in charge," Trace replied easily, already heading for the door. "In the meantime, you might as well take your time, drying your hair and getting warmed up and stuff, 'cause it's going to be a while before the boys are done."

He walked out, shutting the door behind him.

Susannah stared at the closed bedroom door, then picked up her hair dryer, and the pile of clothes and headed for the adjacent bathroom.

Max had gone all out on the house, she thought as she peeled off the soaking-wet clothes. The second floor had six bedrooms, all with their own bath. Four were decorated in masculine motifs. Trace had told her that he was staying in the master suite at the other end of the house.

She was in what appeared to be the guest room. There was a fireplace at one end. An emerald-green silk bedspread covered the comfortable queen-size bed. A beautiful Persian rug covered the center of the polished wood floors. One corner of the room had been turned into a cozy reading nook, complete with armchair, lamp and bookshelves filled with current fiction.

There were worse places to be. Besides, she needed a few minutes to warm up and collect herself before the evening ahead, she thought as she glanced around at the deep whirlpool tub, and separate glass-walled shower stall. And the best way to do that would be to sink into a hot bubble bath up to her chin.

"SINCE WHEN did you start drinking tea, Dad?" Nate asked as he put the cleaning supplies and pail back in the kitchen broom closet.

"I didn't," Trace replied casually as he waited for the kettle to heat. "This is for Susannah." Max had obviously remembered, too. Hence, the selection of fruit teas up in the cupboard, along with the Colombian-roast coffee Trace preferred.

"Oh." Nate watched his dad prepare a tray, then said, "Listen, I'm sorry about earlier. We kind of got carried away."

Trace nodded, readily accepting his son's apology. "Next time you feel like being rowdy, do it outside."

"Okay. Tell Susannah I'm sorry she was hit."

"Will do, but it wouldn't hurt for you to say so, too, when you get a chance."

Nate lingered. "Are you still in love with Susannah?"

Trace paused. "Why would you ask that?"

"Remember when Mom died? You said that once you love someone, the love is always there, in your heart. That it never goes away, even if the person does. So I wondered, if you loved Susannah once, and you must've if you married her, right?"

"Right."

"Then you must still love her," Nate continued, looking at Trace for confirmation. "Right?"

"It's complicated," Trace said finally.

"You always say that when you don't know somethin'," Jason said, joining his brother and father in the kitchen.

"In this case," Trace admitted honestly as Susannah's boys wandered in, too, their clothes still damp and sticking to them, their faces still blackened. "It's true. Susannah and I haven't seen each other for years. We were friends once. We loved each other once."

"You also got divorced," Scott interjected quietly, shoving both hands into the pockets of his jeans.

"We were young," Trace said simply. "And as it turned out, not as mature as we should have been. The bottom line is, we didn't communicate very well. Maybe if we had, we would have stayed together. Maybe we would have split, anyway. It's hard to know." *I guess Max wants us to find out.*

"So what next?" Jason piped up.

"We take it one day, one minute, at a time. And in the meantime—" Trace looked at all four boys with an honesty he felt they would all appreciate "—we all try a lot harder to get along."

"I THOUGHT I SMELLED raspberry tea." Susannah bounded into the kitchen a few minutes later.

She was wearing jeans and a sweatshirt that molded her supple curves in the way only old soft clothes can. Socks and terry-cloth slippers, instead of sneakers. She had dried her glossy sable brown hair into a fluffy bob around her face. She smelled of an intoxicating mixture of soap and White Linen. Trace could tell from the heightened color in her face that she had just emerged from a hot steamy bath. Just looking at her, standing beside her, brought back a wealth of memories. It had been a long time since he had seen her emerge from a bubble bath....

He turned his attention back to the tea he was making. "I thought you could use some."

"Very perceptive of you." She poured herself a cup, added a spoonful of sugar and leaned against the counter. Though his mind was on how enticingly beautiful she looked, he could tell from the purposeful expression on her face, and the set of her shoulders, that her mind was clearly on their four boys and the evening ahead. "About dinner," she began earnestly.

"We could drive into town and eat at Pearl's."

Susannah took a sip of her tea and, still considering his suggestion, glanced in the fridge. "It'll be faster to feed them here. Let's see. Lettuce, tomato, ground beef, cheese. We've got fresh rolls, plenty of potatoes, milk and ice cream. Do your boys like cheeseburgers, fries and chocolate milkshakes?"

Trace had to admit it, Susannah sure knew the way to a young man's heart. His, too. He smiled at her, wondering all the while what his life would've been like if she had only been his wife all this time. "They love 'em."

"Then that's what we'll have. Not exactly a dietician's delight, considering the cholesterol count, but it'll make them happy, and tonight I think we could all use a little comfort food and tender loving care."

Trace couldn't help noting she had included herself in the tally. He lounged against the counter and watched her take another lengthy sip of her tea. "You feeling okay?"

Susannah set her cup aside and sprang into action, pulling ingredients from the refrigerator right and left. "Why wouldn't I?"

Trace watched her bend over to get the lettuce, tomato and onions from the vegetable bin. He admired the curve of her bottom beneath the snug-fitting jeans. "Sometimes those water balloons pack a mean punch." He hated to think of her hurting anywhere.

Her arms full of food she intended to prepare, Susannah closed the refrigerator with her hip. She dumped the food on the counter, and stood on tiptoe to reach two of the copper-bottomed skillets from the hanging rack overhead. "You asking that out of curiosity or from personal experience?"

Trace stepped in to help her get the skillets off the hook. "I admit to throwing and being hit by a few in my time," he said, smiling at her as their bodies collided then moved apart. Aware he was still in his suit pants, white shirt and tie, he remarked, "You look surprised."

Susannah shrugged one slender shoulder. Her eyes moved to his then skittered away. "I admit I have a hard time imagining you goofing off, ever." She moved to the back door. Seeing a gas grill on the deck overlooking Silver Lake, she smiled. "You were always so serious," she continued conversationally as she headed back to the counter.

"Not always." Trace joined her at the sink. "I can remember before my parents died. Things were a lot different."

She waited until they were both finished washing their hands, then handed him a dish towel, their fingers touching lightly in the process. "You were what...fourteen when it happened?" she asked.

Trace nodded. He joined her at the center island and helped her form the ground meat into hamburger patties that they placed on a glass tray. "Patience was twelve. Cody was six. At that point, we were a pretty rowdy group, ourselves." Trace grinned fondly as he recalled the only carefree time he had ever known. "We used to pull pranks on each other all the time. In fact, we often exasperated Mom and Dad because we goofed around so much. I remember when they went down to Mexico together, on that last trip so that Dad could demonstrate the new surgical technique he was developing, along with Mom's help. Before they left, they cautioned us to behave for our baby-sitter. They were only going to be gone a couple of days.''

''Then the earthquake hit,'' she said. Finished making the hamburgers, they washed their hands again, and began working on the vegetables.

Trace nodded as he cut the potatoes into fries. ''You remember the details, don't you?'' She acknowledged that she did and he went on. ''They got out okay when the building they were in collapsed,'' he reflected, unable to believe how much the loss of his parents still hurt, even after all this time. ''But they went back in to help save others. And that's when they were killed in the falling debris.''

Susannah drew a breath, the empathy she felt for what he had been through reflected on her pretty face. Somehow, Trace ruminated, though it did nothing at all to change things or in any way alter his loss, her simple gesture of compassion helped.

She wiped her hands on a towel and touched his arm gently. Trace sighed, his mood turning bleakly introspective once again. For a moment, he concentrated on cutting the potatoes. Aware Susannah was waiting for him to speak, he forced himself to push on, to tell her the things he hadn't been able to bring himself to talk about when they were married, because the wounds had still been too raw, too fresh, he too immature to know how to handle them well. ''Max came to our home, and I knew, even before he took me and Patience aside and told us what had happened and that Mom and Dad were among the missing.'' Trace found himself running short of breath, so he had to pause and inhale deeply.

He went back to slicing potatoes with extraordinary care, while Susannah continued to peel them in much the same, ultracautious way. ''Max told us that our parents had last been seen trying to help others, which made sense since Dad was a doctor and Mom was a nurse, and neither of them would have ever turned away from anyone in need of medical assistance.'' Trace fell silent a moment, recalling the mixture of shock, grief and fear that had all but immobilized him.

Again, he forced himself to push on. He knew it was therapeutic to talk about his loss, especially on the heels of yet another. ''Max felt Cody was too young to be told anything, until we knew for sure what had happened to Mom and Dad. And he asked me to try and hold it together for Patience, so Cody wouldn't be upset unnecessarily. I agreed. And that was the end of my carefree youth.''

Trace paused, watching as Susannah moved to the sink and began washing lettuce and tomatoes. Wanting to be just as casual, he concentrated on peeling a red onion. ''A few days later, when we learned the worst had happened and my parents had been killed, I had even more responsibility. I knew Mom and Dad would've expected me to take care of both Patience and Cody. And Max, because he had never married or had any children of his own, needed a lot of help, too. I think at that point in time, I grew up in just a couple of days.''

"So," Susannah concluded softly as she spread the cleaned, sliced vegetables on a serving platter with efficient ease, "no more play for you."

Trace added the onions, and watched as she covered the tray with plastic wrap and slid it back into the refrigerator to chill. "Not until I had kids of my own." Glad to be on safer emotional ground, he added informatively, "Speaking of whom, I think you and I have our work cut out for us if we're going to make the next forty-eight hours, never mind the years after that, work."

Susannah raised an eyebrow, whether in mild agreement of his assessment or simple wariness, Trace couldn't be sure. "It's going to be odd, living together—" Susannah drew a shaky breath.

He watched as she lifted the platter of meat, switched on the lantern-style deck lights and headed out the French doors to the rough-hewn deck overlooking Silver Lake. Moonlight glimmered on the surface of the water. A gentle breeze blew across the lake, stirring the crisp clean air, and reminding them just how cool it could get at night in this part of Montana, even in June.

"I know." He turned on the gas grill, and adjusted the flame, while below them, the sounds of cicadas and bullfrogs could be heard.

Susannah put the platter of burgers on the grill. Together, they waited for the briquettes to heat up. "But maybe if we make a team effort—" she supposed.

"It's the only way," Trace agreed with deep-seated practicality as he followed her over to the edge of the low-set deck. He propped a hip against the railing and stared at her. The darkness of night had never enchanted him before. Now, he found it suddenly very romantic to be standing out here in the summer evening with her, the granite mountains rising in the distance on the other side of the lake, and stars shining in a black velvet sky overhead. "I'll lead, of course."

Susannah had been looking out at the lake, a dreamy expression on her face. At his proclamation, she whirled toward him, as suddenly as if she had been given an electric shock. "What do you mean, you'll lead?" she demanded incredulously.

Trace shrugged, his mind made up about that much, even if she did intend to argue. "One of us has to," he explained practically. "And since I'm the dad—"

"Wait a minute, Trace," Susannah interrupted. "I am not—I repeat, *not* one of your subordinates." She propped both her hands on her slender hips. "You handle your boys. I'll handle mine."

Trace blew out a gusty breath, wondering all the while how he ever could have forgotten, even for one second, what an exasperating woman Susannah could be when she set her mind to it. "That will never work if we are going to successfully combine households, Susannah," he told her firmly. His tranquil gaze zeroed in on her incredibly long-lashed, sable brown eyes. "We're going to be living in *one* house. We ought to have *one* set of rules." And they would be his.

Susannah drew a breath. "In case you haven't noticed, we seem to have two totally different styles of parenting, Trace," she said humorlessly. "And probably two very different sets of rules, too."

Trace agreed grimly. "I've noticed. And for the record, Susannah, you are way too lax with your boys. You let them get away with murder, negotiate practically everything, even offer to help them clean up the irresponsible messes they make. Which in turn just encourages such frat-house behavior like water-balloon fights inside the house. Keep it up and they are going to walk right over you.''

Susannah flushed bright red. "Yes, well, you are too strict," she retorted, giving him no quarter, either. "You bark out orders like a drill sergeant, insist this house be kept like a boot-camp barracks and you tolerate no chicanery at all, which, I might add, all boys that age need a little of in their lives. Heck, everyone does! Hence, your boys went overboard with the water-balloon shenanigans tonight because they were probably never cut loose before in their lives. If you keep up that nonstop strictness, heaven only knows where it will lead."

Trace hated to admit it, but his sons had been awfully solemn. Not always, mind you, just since their mother had died and he had found himself having to really scramble to keep things together. Just as he was scrambling now. It worried and annoyed him to realize that he may have inadvertently put his boys in the same spot he had been in upon his own parents' death.

"Keep your voice down," he told Susannah quietly, worried about upsetting the kids this evening any more than they had been, with the announcement about the will and their impending marriage. Deciding the grill could wait, he dropped his voice to a chastising whisper. "Do you want the boys to know we're fighting about this? Especially since in a couple of days, we'll have to tell them we've decided to combine households not just for forty-eight hours, but permanently?''

Susannah rolled her eyes in obvious exasperation. Once again, Trace noted despairingly, it seemed they agreed on very little.

"It will not kill them to know we disagree on something, whether we combine households or not," she stated emphatically. "Furthermore, I am not the same person you married, Trace." Her eyes narrowed as she watched him loosen the knot of his silk tie, then, scowling in frustration, take it off altogether. Still pursing her soft sexy lips in indignation, she watched as he tossed it down on the redwood picnic table. "And I am not going to pretend it is okay with me for you to completely take over our life together, when it is not okay with me at all!"

Trace frowned. He could see her digging in her heels. This was not going at all the way he had planned. But it was not for lack of trying on his part. Considering how she had deceived him, and left him out of the first sixteen—count 'em—sixteen years of his son's life, he thought he was being extremely reasonable. And accommodating. Loosening the top two buttons on his shirt, he strode forward until they were standing toe to toe, and stood, looking down at her. "I am not the same person you married, either, Susannah," he announced with the kind of dead-on implacability that characteristically had his employees and his children standing at attention. "These days," he continued to tell her with a steadfastness that made her shiver, "I leave nothing—" especially my personal relationships, he added silently "—to chance."

Whirling away from him once again, Susannah paced the deck, the breeze blowing her hair in a soft halo around her pretty face. "Well, I have news for you, Trace," she stormed, ignoring his cool disregard and waving her arms to effectively and defiantly punctuate her words. "You can't orchestrate everything. Not about your life alone, or my life alone, or our life together," she finished, arrowing an index finger in the direction of his chest.

It annoyed him to see her looking as though she wanted to walk out on him again. It irritated him even more to think he might lose her before he'd had a chance to enjoy being with her again, or somehow make things right—with her, with Scott, the child he'd never known he had, even with their failed marriage.

"Want to bet?" Trace gave in to impulse and tugged her into his arms. A stunned expression flashed on her face as he tunneled his hands in her hair and brought her mouth up to his, a brief whiff of her perfume seemed to caress him, and then all was forgotten as he was completely caught up in the sensation of her lips against his.

He had always wanted her, even at the end, even when their marriage was over. Even so, it had never been like this, he thought as she threaded her hands through his hair and passionately returned his kiss. Desire flowed through him in hot waves and he kissed her long and hard and deep. He kissed her until she clung to him and moaned softly and melted in his arms. He was amazed at the depth of his arousal, the intensity of his feelings. Susannah was so beautiful she took his breath away. In all the years they had been apart, he had thought—hoped—he had forgotten what she did to him. Instead, the passion he felt for her—had always felt—had only gotten stronger...along with his equally entrenched desire to take her and make her his, and only his.

Susannah knew she shouldn't be giving in to temptation this way. But it had been so long, she thought, since she had been really loved, touched, held, or kissed. So long since she had felt like a woman, and not just a mom. As Trace's kiss turned unbearably sweet, intimate and seductive, as his arms swept down her back, to bring her even closer to the uncompromising warmth and heat of his tall frame, she couldn't say no, couldn't resist—couldn't seem to do anything but move closer still. And that was when it happened. When she heard the sound of the patio door slamming open behind them. The clatter of feet. Then several shocked gasps and one very loud, very indignant male voice behind them. "Hey! We thought there was gonna be no sex!"

Chapter Five

"Guess we were wrong," Scott drawled as Susannah and Trace flushed and broke apart.

"And how," Nate agreed.

"Unless they're administering mouth-to-mouth resuscitation to each other," Jason kidded.

Beside them, Mickey blinked. It was clear he still didn't know what was going on. "Well?" he asked finally, turning to the other boys for confirmation, like the baby of the family that he was. "Is this sex or isn't it?" he demanded plaintively.

Susannah's oldest child exchanged looks with Trace's oldest son. "Well, Mom?" Scott echoed.

"And Dad?" Nate echoed, picking up the thread with the same witty determination.

"What's going on?" Scott asked, his deep blue eyes narrowing as he, too, apparently tried to decide the import of finding his mother in her ex-husband and coinheritor's arms.

Susannah flushed all the more, for once in her life so embarrassed she was completely at a loss. Trace, she could not help noting humorously, did not appear to be faring much better.

"Actually," she began.

"The grill is about ready, I think," Trace said. He turned around to put the hamburgers on.

"You're not getting out of this that easily, Dad," Nate said.

Susannah knew the boys deserved some explanation, but was just not sure what that should be. "It was—"

"—just a kiss for old time's sake," Trace finished for her.

She turned to glance at him, so only he could see the look in her eyes. It had felt like more than that to her.

Trace cleared his throat. "We, uh, we're sorry if we alarmed you by getting a little carried away, but..." He cleared his throat again and gave the boys all looks that were strictly man-to-man. "Sometimes that happens."

I'll say, Susannah thought.

She turned to Mickey, figuring since Trace had taken it upon himself to answer for both of them, he could field all further questions for both of them, too. At least from the older boys. There were some things her youngest did not need to hear. "Mickey, honey, would you come in the kitchen with me? I need someone to help line up celery and carrot sticks on a tray."

"Okay." Mickey fell into step beside her. "So," he asked importantly as he shoved his hands into the pockets of his jeans and they went inside the house. "What is all this kissing stuff about, anyway?"

"ENOUGH ABOUT the birds and the bees and the-time-and-season-for-everything stuff. I still don't get why you and Trace were kissing, Mom," Mickey said impatiently ten minutes later as he painstakingly added black and green olives to the sliced vegetables on the relish tray. "What does it mean?"

Good question, Susannah thought as she turned the sizzling fries with a slotted spoon.

"Does it mean you like each other? That you're boyfriend and girlfriend? What?"

Seeing that the French fries were done, Susannah removed them from the skillet and spread them out on paper towels to drain. "It means we were once married, and now, because of Max's will, we're going to be again."

"But are you friends?" Mickey persisted doggedly.

"We're trying to be."

"Good friends? Boyfriend and girlfriend? Sleep-over pals, what?"

"People who are Mom and Trace's age aren't supposed to be sleep-over pals," Scott informed his younger brother as he came through the door, carrying the charbroiled burgers. Trace, Nate and Jason were fast on his heels and listening intently. "Not unless they're married, anyway," Scott continued. "At least that's what Mom always says. She wants us to wait until we're married to sleep over with someone of the opposite sex. In our case, Mickey, that would be girls," Scott explained patiently. "But since Mom and Trace are going to be married again, and they were already married before, that kind of muddles things. At least that's what I think they would tell you if they could get their tongues untied long enough to do so." Scott looked at Susannah, long and hard. "Or am I wrong?"

"I think that about sums it up," Susannah murmured self-consciously, wondering when their roles had switched and Scott had suddenly become the responsible one, she the romantically reckless "teenager."

"Me, too," Trace agreed firmly, before breaking into a broad smile. "And that being the case, I say we eat."

ALL SIX GATHERED around the big oak table in the country kitchen of the log-cabin lake house. To Susannah's relief, no sooner had they said grace and filled their plates, than the talk turned to fishing. "You mean you guy's never fished in a mountain stream?" Nate asked her two sons.

"No. Have you?" Scott asked, looking very interested.

"All the time," Nate enthused. "We know some great places for trout, right on the Silver Spur. And there's some really fine white water, too. Jason and I can show it to you and Mickey tomorrow, if you want."

"The fishing is okay. You know where the approved places are," Trace said. "If you guys behave yourselves, and Susannah and I both agree it's okay, timing-wise and so on, you all can go. But stay away from the white water, unless I'm there with you. It's dangerous."

His boys looked disappointed but did not argue. Apparently, this was a family rule, one she approved of.

"Can we go in the morning then?" Scott asked Susannah.

"Actually, I was counting on your help tomorrow morning. They're going to be shorthanded over at the logging camp dining hall. I thought maybe you and Mickey could bus tables for me during the breakfast shift." Susannah turned to Trace. "Unfortunately, that means you'll have to go, too, since I'll be there from 5:00 a.m. to 9:00 a.m."

"And so will Nate and Jason." Trace volunteered his sons cheerfully. "They can bus tables, too."

All four boys looked less than thrilled.

"Work before play, guys," Trace reminded them.

There was some good-natured grumbling all around. And then once again the talk turned to the wilds of Montana, and the quarter-million acres of timberland that Trace and Susannah were jointly inheriting from Uncle Max.

"IF YOU HAVE to get up at 4:00 a.m. to get to work by five, I think you'd better get to bed now," Susannah told her sons once the dishes were finished.

"Morning will be here before you know it," Trace told his sons.

Nate and Scott exchanged hopelessly pained looks. "Doesn't sound as if they're giving us much choice, does it?" Scott drawled.

"Nah, but then that's parents," Nate agreed as he and Scott headed for the stairs, their two younger brothers not far behind. "Always giving orders."

"Especially mine."

"Not as much as mine."

"Wanna bet?"

Their voices trailed off. Susannah glanced at her watch. Hard to believe it was already ten o'clock. Morning would come soon. Probably too soon, judging by how tired she was. "I guess I better go up, too."

Trace caught her wrist and tugged her toward him so suddenly she collided with his chest. "How about a walk down to the lakeshore first?"

To her irritation, it seemed more an order than a request. Knowing how determined he was, that the boys were just upstairs, perhaps even within earshot, had her tempering her reaction to his typically autocratic behavior. Trying hard not to notice how warm her wrist was beneath his light staying grip, or the way the rest of her was suddenly tingling, she angled her head up at his. Clearly, from the I-know-you-better-than-you-know-yourself glint in his deep blue eyes, Trace had plans for them both. "I've seen it," she said. Then mentally added, "From a distance."

"I know, but I think we need to talk."

"OKAY, what is it?" Susannah demanded shortly as they reached the boat dock.

There were so many reasons that she shouldn't let this keep happening, she thought. The primary one being that the more time she spent with him, especially like this, one-on-one, the more she felt as if she was already married to him again. Not in name only, but deep inside. And that was crazy. They had been apart for almost seventeen years.

Though they were in clear view of the back of the lake house, their silhouettes clearly illuminated by the electric lanterns that bordered the dock, they were well out of earshot of the house, and were therefore reassured of some degree of privacy.

As straightforward as always, Trace got right down to business. "I think we may need to revise our plans."

Although he was acting as if it were no big deal for them to be out here alone, her pulse was pounding at his nearness. She could see the five-o'clock shadow lining his handsome face and knew firsthand how deliciously abrasive it would feel against her face, were she to end up in his arms once again.

But that, she reassured herself firmly, was not going to happen. This time, she would proceed far more cautiously and keep him at arm's length. "What do you mean revise them?" she demanded. "We barely made them."

"The boys are not buying our only-friends, routine."

Susannah rolled her eyes. Not about to let him know how he was getting to her, she retorted dryly, "Maybe if you stopped kissing me at every opportunity—"

They'd been together only a matter of hours and he'd already kissed her twice. So what if chemistry like theirs came along once in a lifetime. That didn't mean they had to act on it. Never mind make up for all the time they had been apart....

His glance took her in from head to toe before returning to settle on her lips. "Maybe if you stopped responding like a house afire."

"So I'm flesh and blood. So some residual chemistry still exists between us after all these years," she fibbed, deliberately downplaying what she felt whenever he was near her. "So what?" She stood apart from him, enjoying the feel of the cool evening breeze sifting off the lake.

"So, sooner or later, that fire of ours is going to burn out of control, unless we do something about it."

Keeping her eyes fastened on his, Susannah drew in a wealth of crisp, clean air. "Is that so?"

"Yes."

"And what, pray tell, do you propose to do about that?"

He shrugged and shoved his hands into the pockets of his suit pants. "Let it burn out of control."

Susannah blinked, the irony of the situation not lost on her. She had left Trace once because he didn't have time for her or their marriage; now, he couldn't seem to stop micromanaging the details of each. The corners of her mouth lifted wryly. "Excuse me?"

He stepped so close she could feel his body heat. "The boys have noticed our passion. We already know we're not just going to get married according to the terms of Max's will, but stay married as a way of sharing custody of Scott. It's pretty clear our boys are going to want to know what the reason for that is. And since we can't give them the real reason, we're going to have to come up with something else, something they will accept."

Susannah folded her hands in front of her and took a calming breath. "And you think that reason is going to be sex."

His eyes gleamed with sudden practicality. "Like you said, some residual passion still exists between us. The boys have already witnessed it firsthand."

Exasperation stiffened her spine. "So you want us to tell them what?" She flung her arms out to her sides. "That we're so crazy in lust we can't keep our hands off each other?"

He shrugged his broad shoulders again and ran a hand through the short, precisely-cut layers of his wheat-gold hair. "It's not far from the truth."

Susannah dug her feet into the softness of the thick manicured grass. She gave him a withering glare and started to move past. "Speak for yourself."

He put out a hand to bar her way. "You saw for yourself this evening they're already confused. If we get married, and delay getting divorced, ostensibly to inherit according to the terms of Max's will, our reasoning may work for a while—as long as we keep our hands off each other. Which, given the way things are already going, I might add, seems highly unlikely."

As much as she was loath to admit it, she was afraid he was right about that. She looked down her nose at him. "What is your point?"

"My point is, we should be forthright with the boys about our plans, as soon as we can. We should also tell them as much of the truth as we can."

"The truth being that we still desire each other," Susannah guessed as her blood warmed even more.

"And hence have decided to stay married, now that the fires of our love are rekindled. That way, it all works out neatly," Trace explained, obviously already having given the matter some thought. "We get married as planned, thereby honoring Max's wishes. We inherit. Meanwhile, we sort of show and tell the boys we have fallen for each other all over again. And therefore have decided to stay married and combine households," he finished in the same pleasant and infallible tone he had always used to make a sales pitch to a client.

Remembering how he'd always put his relationship with her and their life together last on his priority list, Susannah tensed. "Kind of like a business deal, right?"

Trace shrugged. "If that's the way you want to look at it."

It wasn't.

He studied the impassive look on her face. "I know this isn't romantic," he said. "I know how much you always liked things to be romantic in the past, Susannah. But in this case, we have no choice."

She had heard that before, too, many times. It always ended in her being hurt. She quirked a discerning eyebrow at him. "Don't we?" She might owe him time with Scott, the opportunity to catch up on all he had missed. But that was all she owed him.

"Maybe if you had come to me years earlier, things would've been different," he said in a soft reasonable tone that set her teeth on edge.

"Right." She trod nearer, her feet sinking ever deeper into the thick velvety lawn. "Had I only done that, you wouldn't have had to punish me by forcing me into marriage now. You could have done it then. Or, had I refused to cooperate with you, you could have just taken Scott away from me at the outset."

Trace's lips thinned unhappily. "I won't deny I would have tried to talk you into coming back, had you only told me you were pregnant," he admitted harshly.

"And if that had failed?"

"I would have fought for my son. Accepted no less than joint custody."

Susannah nodded grimly. "Exactly as I thought." She had known Trace would be ruthless when it came to getting what he wanted. And that was what scared her.

"Which is another reason why you never told me about the baby," he concluded, reciprocal anger flashing across his handsome face.

"I admit I didn't want Scott to be the prize in a tug-of-war between us." She hadn't wanted their baby to be wanted only for the challenge of hanging on to him. She knew from experience that Trace looked at things as goals to be obtained. Once he had met his objectives, he tended to move right on to the next project he'd set for himself.

That was how he had built a business empire for himself, in only seventeen years. Why he had neglected her almost from the moment the ink was dry on their marriage certificate. Because once he had wooed, won and married her, he had considered their relationship a fait accompli. Hence, having conquered her, he could set his sights on other challenges.

She wasn't sure she could go back to that, even if theirs was to be little more than a marriage of convenience this time, without having her heart broken all over again.

"And Scott still shouldn't be caught up in this battle between us," Trace said quietly, reacting as the loving and compassionate father he was. "So what do you say? Will you heat things up between us, at least on the surface, for the boys' sake, so that when we do tell them we intend to stay married, it won't be such a shock to them?"

Susannah thought of the questions Mickey had asked, and the way Scott, Nate and Jason had been slyly sizing up everything she and Trace did and said.

Trace was right. They did need to do something, if only to put the boys' minds at ease. She sighed in defeat. "When are you asking we do this?"

"The optimum time would be sometime before the ceremony takes place."

"YOU'RE MOVING awfully fast, even for you, expecting me to start sharing your bedroom and being the loving wife for all the world to see in less than forty hours."

Trace knew he was taking advantage, not just of the situation, but of her. He couldn't help it. Whenever conceivable, he liked things to be wrapped up as quickly as possible.

Right now, with so much at stake and so little resolved, he felt as if he were living life on a razor's edge. "And it's not as if we've never been married before, Susannah. We have been," he said persuasively.

As if prior experience were all that counted! Susannah thought hotly. "Yes, but back then there was a difference," she countered sweetly. "Back then, you were never home." This time around, because of the kids, she had the feeling that would not be the case.

"I've changed," he admitted. "I have responsibilities to my children, and so do you."

If only he'd felt a similar sense of responsibility toward his wife. But maybe that was unfair, Susannah thought. She didn't know what kind of husband he had been the second time around. Nor did she know what kind of husband he would make for her now that he was thirty-eight instead of twenty-one. Certainly, they were both more mature. Trace at least a little more sensitive, though clearly just as driven to succeed.

"I have to think about this," Susannah said.

"There's nothing to think about."

There it was again, his lord-of-the-manor attitude. As always, it grated on her nerves. "Maybe not from your point of view," she asserted with an inner calm she didn't feel.

"What's that supposed to mean?"

"Not all of us view marriage as just another business deal or convenience, Trace." Susannah splayed a trembling hand across her chest, annoyed at the way he already seemed to be taking her for granted once again. "Some of us approach marriage with our hearts."

Trace sighed impatiently and braced his hands on his waist. "Someone has to think ahead and solve the problems as they come up. Like it or not, the boys are confused about the way we've been behaving, and probably will continue to behave. They stand to get even more confused unless we come up with a logical story that will make all our actions seem plausible. Turning our story into a modern, mostly male version of "The Brady Bunch" meets *A Love That Never Died* will do just that."

As much as she was loath to agree with him, he had a point. Susannah knew she owed him time with Scott. And she did not want to upset the boys. Going into the arrangement any other way would confuse and upset them all the more. Scott particularly was already suspicious. She didn't want him to start investigating the circumstances and dates surrounding his birthday and the end of her marriage to Trace. If he did, there would be no hiding the truth from him.

"The boys might even find it amusing, to see us making goo-goo eyes at each other," Trace continued, searching her face.

Aware he was once again weighing and analyzing her every move, Susannah said, "I'm sure you do."

He grew very still and Susannah knew in a flash that at least in his opinion, she had gone too far. "What's that supposed to mean?" Trace demanded.

Susannah shrugged one slender shoulder. Without warning, she felt herself getting hot all over. "I left your bed when you would've preferred I stay. Now, I'm coming back to your bed, at least in a figurative sense, when I would prefer to stay out of it. Rather ironic, wouldn't you say?" she queried sweetly, the heat racing along her skin intensifying to a fever pitch. She looked directly into his eyes. "Not to mention the perfect revenge."

Was that what she'd thought of the kisses they had shared? Trace wondered in stunned amazement. Revenge? He knew if that's what she believed, he would have to do better. Susannah was a very passionate woman. Instinct told him she wouldn't lock herself into a marriage with him unless she was convinced of the genuineness of his desire for her, and vice versa. Fortunately, that was the one area, the only area, of their relationship where they had never had a problem, Trace thought with something akin to relief. All he had to do was remind her of that. And on that score, luck was also with him, giving him an opportunity he could not, would not, ignore. "Don't look now," he said quietly, inclining his head slightly at the rear of the lake house, "but we have an audience."

Susannah froze. He could tell by the chagrin in her expression that she already thought she knew the answer even before she croaked, "Where?"

"The upstairs bedroom windows. I count—" Trace narrowed his eyes as he stepped closer to murmur in her ear "—one, two, three, four faces." Knowing there was no better time to demonstrate their growing attraction to each other to the boys than during this moonlit scene next to the lake, Trace gathered Susannah into his arms and tugged her close so that every inch of her was feeling every inch of him. Ignoring her soft gasp of dismay, he lowered his head and fastened his lips over hers. And suddenly found, as the need poured out of her, mingling with the desire and the lingering hurt, that she was not the only one whose heart was pounding like thunder in her chest. Her lips were hot and sweet and soft. And so seductive. Totally caught up in what he was feeling, he threaded a hand through her hair and tilted her head so that he could delve even farther into her mouth. His need to be close to her was as overwhelming as it was surprising. And he knew that even if he kissed her and held her and made wild, reckless love to her one thousand times, it would still not be enough. It would never be enough. No matter what she'd done to him.

Susannah moaned as Trace flattened his hand over her spine, urging her closer, until her breasts were against his chest. As her mouth opened to his, he kissed her long and hard and deep, with a mastery and tenderness he hadn't possessed in his youth. She had never felt anything like this in her life, never wanted anyone so much as she wanted him at that moment. And that was when she knew it had to end. Before he had her convincing herself this was love, and not lust-filled revenge.

Her mouth tingling, her whole body aching with a yearning that went soul-deep, she moved back slightly. She was dizzy, shaking. In direct contrast, he seemed as calm and in control as ever. He seemed to think, she decided unhappily as she studied the implacable expression on his handsome face, that they were only indulging in the inevitable.

And that, she knew, was not the case.

Nothing was certain, yet, especially her feelings.

Releasing her, Trace glanced surreptitiously at the house. Recalling abruptly what had precipitated their fiery embrace, Susannah followed suit. Somehow, she thought with a beleaguered sigh, she wasn't surprised to see four shadowy figures still standing at the window some fifty yards away, their youthful faces and hands glued to the panes in a posture of absolute astonishment.

With a great deal of effort, she stifled a moan of utter dismay. "They're still watching," she murmured, flushing with embarrassment and feeling like a very bad actor in a stage play. The kind who couldn't keep his or her real feelings separate from the ones he or she was supposed to be conveying to the audience.

"Don't I know it," Trace murmured back. His sensual lips curving in masculine satisfaction, his gaze resting hotly on her damp, kiss-swollen lips, Trace reached up and smoothed a strand of hair from her cheek. In the gentle glow of the dock lights, his eyes radiated a mixture of triumph and pleasure.

Wordlessly, he tucked the strand of errant silk behind her ear. "A few more clinches like that, a few adoring looks, and no one—not even our kids or my brother and sister—will question why we've decided to make our marriage a real one," he said.

Chapter Six

"What kind of pancakes did you say these were?"

"Whole-wheat banana-walnut." Susannah smiled at the burly loggers going through the cafeteria-style line.

"Does this mean no more plain ol' buttermilk pancakes?"

"Oh, we'll have buttermilk," Susannah was quick to reassure. "And blueberry. And apple-cinnamon, and strawberry, and any other kind of hotcakes I can dream up. The point is to give you fellas more variety, so you don't feel you're eating the same old thing day in, day out. Think you can live with that?"

"If everything tastes as good as this breakfast does, you betcha!" another logger, who had cleaned his plate and was getting up to head back to the line for seconds, called out.

"You said this was turkey bacon?"

"Uh-huh." Susannah smiled warmly.

"Tastes a lot better than I figured on."

"What kind of potatoes?" asked another.

"Onion-pepper hash browns."

"And the juice?"

"Orange-peach."

"This is darn good, Ms. Hart."

"Call me, Susannah. And thank you." Susannah headed down the rows of tables, handing out questionnaires and pencils right and left. "Don't forget to fill out your menu requests before you leave, please, so I'll know what kinds of things you like."

Watching from the adjacent cafeteria office, where he had settled down to go over the latest financial reports of the company he was inheriting from Max, Trace was amazed at how adroitly Susannah handled not just the loggers, but the whole operation. She had waltzed in at 5:00 a.m., dragging her crew of five sleepy males behind her, and hadn't stopped since. First cooking, with the help of Gillian Taylor and three of the nine part-time cooks the cafeteria employed; supervising the boys as they readied the tables and put out the glassware, dishes and silverware; and then serving and interacting with the men.

She was really in her element here, he thought, and never more so than when surrounded by a bevy of admiring males. It irritated him to see the other men shooting her love-struck glances. It annoyed him even more to realize how jealous he was, and that deep inside, where it really counted, there was a part of him that still considered her his woman, even after all this time.

"You can come out and have some breakfast, too," Susannah said to him from the doorway.

Trace frowned at the message that popped up on his computer screen, that signaled he had just received an electronic-mail message from one Sam Farraday. "Thanks. I'll be there in a minute." His eyes still on the computer screen, Trace clicked into the document. His spirits plummeted as he read the message.

From the doorway, Susannah was still tracking his every movement. "Problem?" she asked.

Trace scowled. "Sam Farraday is having second thoughts about selling me the Farraday Timber operation."

Susannah's sable brown eyes widened. "That's a problem?"

"You're damn right it is." Trace scowled. "My attorney just finished drawing up the final papers for me. They were supposed to be signed later this afternoon."

Thrusting her hands into the pockets of her white chef's apron, Susannah edged closer. Trace caught a whiff of her perfume as she perched on the edge of the desk. "And now Farraday is backing out," she concluded, still studying him intently.

"That's not going to happen."

Susannah rubbed at a spot of flour on the knee of her jeans, her fingertips moving in slow circular motions until the flour blended into the fabric. Finished, she looked back up at him. "How can you be so sure?"

Trace's throat was parched. He reached for the cup of coffee he had brought into the office with him. "Because I have worked damn hard on this deal," he told her, not bothering to hide his confidence that all would work out eventually. "And I need that timber." And he wasn't going to give up until he got it.

With a soft, unconscious motion, Susannah tucked the bobbed ends of her hair behind her ear. "What's so special about the Farraday Timber operation?"

"They've got western white pine."

"Don't you?"

"No. My company harvests western hemlock and Douglas fir."

"What about Uncle Max's company?"

"Western red cedar and ponderosa pine."

"I don't see the problem. If you already have four varieties of wood—"

"There are five types native to Montana," Trace interrupted as he noted the time Sam Farraday's e-mail message had been sent. It said shortly after midnight, which was, in Trace's experience, the time of day when people were most likely to have doubts about anything and everything pertaining to business. Often, what seemed unsolvable late at night, seemed completely within one's realm early the next day. Aware Susannah was still regarding him intently, he patiently finished his explanation, "The Farraday operation, when combined with Uncle Max's lumber company, will enable me to produce all five types of timber." And that, Trace thought, was a coup he couldn't ignore.

"What if this Sam Farraday doesn't want to sell?" Susannah persisted matter-of-factly. "Can't you get the western white pine somewhere else?"

"No." Trace exhaled and fixed Susannah with a steady gaze. "Not in that quantity."

Susannah pursed her lips thoughtfully; without lipstick, they looked soft and lusciously full. Recalling with disturbing clarity the kisses they had shared down by the lake the evening before, it was all Trace could do not to pull her into his lap and see if they could duplicate that flash of passion and sensuality once again. "So what are you going to do?" Susannah asked.

Seemingly oblivious to the direction of his thoughts, she toyed with the diamond stud in her ear.

Trace sighed and shoved back his chair. His body humming with a frustration that derived from several different sources, the current difficulties with his work being the least of them, he pushed to his feet. "I am going to make Farraday understand a deal is a deal." Trace's shoulders tensed as he moved around the small office. He hated to be thwarted on any level. He sat back down in front of his laptop computer, already contemplating what his reply to Sam Farraday would be. "We worked for weeks hammering out the terms of the sale," he continued as he began typing his reply to Sam's message with fierce hammerlike strokes. "Sam agreed to this. We even shook on it. So, like it or not, Sam is going to have to follow through."

"SO, WHAT'S GOING on with you and Trace Mc-Kendrick?" Gillian Taylor asked Susannah as the dining hall cleared out and the two of them headed back to the kitchen at the end of the breakfast shift.

Her slender figure encased in hopelessly worn jeans, an oversize man's plaid flannel shirt and boy's Converse-style sneakers, her wildly curling auburn hair caught in a haphazard knot at the nape of her neck, Gillian looked more like a teenage waif than a successful thirty-year-old chef.

She was also Susannah's best friend, and had been ever since Susannah had given her her first job, a place to stay other than the women's shelter where she had been living and helped her get through chef's training. Gillian never talked about her past. Susannah just knew it had been enormously difficult and Gillian was as glad to have it behind her as Susannah was to have the naturally empathetic Gillian for a friend.

Susannah and Gillian, who had yet to eat breakfast, either, took their trays to the butcher block in the center. Susannah pulled up a stool and sat down, while Gillian did the same. Aware she had yet to explain the reason for the sparks flying between Trace and herself, Susannah sighed as she stirred fresh strawberries into a piping-hot dish of cream of wheat, then confided, "He's in his killer business mode again." So what else was new? she wondered discouragingly.

Gillian stirred a generous amount of cream and sugar into her coffee. "What's that?"

"The mode where no one and nothing gets in the way of him getting what he wants."

Gillian—who knew little of Susannah's history with Trace—raised an eyebrow. "Sounds ominous."

Susannah sipped her juice contemplatively. "It usually is."

Gillian, who could eat like a trucker and never gain an ounce, spooned up a forkful of eggs. "You disapprove, I take it?"

"When it comes to getting what he wants, Trace can be very single-minded." And right now, Susannah thought, he didn't just want the Farraday Timber operation, he wanted Scott, and perhaps her, too. That was very unnerving.

Gillian added salt and pepper to her hash browns. "You sound as if you don't approve of his ambition."

Susannah had told herself she was not going to get caught up, playing the same old games, the same old way, with Trace. She shrugged her shoulders. "It's not up to me either to approve or disapprove." Just try and find a way to live with it.

"I see, and yet, according to what I've heard from the boys, you and Trace were spotted kissing just last night," Gillian murmured.

Susannah blushed self-consciously. She should have known that Scott and Mickey, who had been baby-sat by Gillian many a time over the last ten years, would waste no time confiding in her. "There's a reason for that," Susannah said.

"Really?" Gillian slathered butter and jam on a flaky golden biscuit. "I'd like to hear it."

Not wanting either the boys or Trace to overhear, Susannah stood, closed the door that separated the dining hall from the kitchen, sat back down. As they finished their breakfasts, she told Gillian about the terms of Max's will.

"So, you and Trace are going to go for the gusto, huh?" Gillian asked, amazed.

Susannah ran a finger down the side of her tray. "I wouldn't put it that way."

"But both of you do want your inheritances," Gillian insisted.

"Yes."

Gillian sighed as she got up to get them both more coffee. "No wonder he was shooting you all those looks, then," she murmured as she set down Susannah's mug in front of her.

"What looks?" Susannah asked in surprise, stirring cream into her coffee.

Gillian gave Susannah a knowing look. "The love-struck ones."

Susannah flushed. Despite her effort to be cool, calm and collected, she found herself getting embarrassed. "Trace McKendrick is not in love with me," she told Gillian sternly. *Nor was he ever. If he had been, their marriage would have lasted.*

Gillian grinned skeptically and lifted her mug to her lips. "If you say so."

Susannah pushed away from the counter. "I don't want to talk about it." Mug in hand, she pushed open the screen door and stepped outside.

Gillian followed her into the crisp, clean air, also holding her mug. "You don't really have to. I know what I see, on both sides," she relayed as she paced, the pine needles on the ground crunching beneath her tomboy shoes. "Lots and lots of sparks."

The problem was, Susannah thought, she didn't know if those sparks were all for show so that people would not be surprised when she and Trace announced their intention to make their hasty marriage a real one, and not just a means to inherit.

Trace's kisses last night had not felt as if they were for show. They had felt all too real. She'd been up half the night replaying them over and over in her mind. And though she would die before admitting it, she still couldn't stop thinking about how good it felt to be in his arms again. To be near him, even when he annoyed her, which was often. If he kept this up, she knew she was going to have a very hard time resisting him when he finally did make his move, and she knew that time was coming, too. If not before their wedding of convenience, then certainly after, because Trace was not the kind of man who would share a home with a woman, and a life, and not end up making love with her eventually.

And that worried her. She was not the kind of woman who could make love to someone without also giving him her heart.

If only Trace felt the same, it might have been different, but he didn't. To him, there was a clear separation between pleasure and business, and with Trace, business always took center stage. Whether it was the business of reclaiming his son or securing his inheritance or acquiring that Farraday Timber operation he had his eye on, didn't seem to matter. Trace was happy as long as he was chasing some goal.

Susannah did not want to go back to that kind of life. She did not want to be a distant second—or maybe even third or fourth or fifth—in his life. Nor did she want to feel like some obligation to be met. She'd had enough of that with her mother, when she was growing up.

Gillian continued to pace between the row of trees that separated them from the rest of the logging-camp headquarters. "Trace aside, there's something I need to talk to you about."

Susannah heard the undertone of worry in her friend's voice and lifted her chin. "What's the matter?"

"Lots, quite frankly. You said there would be no problems if I took this job," Gillian told Susannah.

Susannah knew how Gillian felt about background checks; because of the secrets in her past, they absolutely undid her. "There isn't anything to worry about, Gillian," Susannah soothed. "Max gave me carte blanche to hire whoever I wanted to run the dining hall. I talked to him about you before he died. He knew you were unwilling to divulge any of the details of your early life, and he was fine with it. Totally cool.''

"Well, someone needs to tell that hotshot lawyer of his,'' Gillian grumbled as she knocked back the rest of her coffee.

"Why? What's Cisco done?'' Susannah couldn't imagine Cisco being rude to anyone.

Gillian released the clip holding her unruly hair at her nape. It tumbled down past her shoulders as she pocketed the clip. "Listen, I've got to go finish getting settled in, if I'm going to start work here full-time on Monday. Are you going to be okay for the rest of the weekend?''

Susannah nodded. "Pearl's Diner is catering the rest of the meals this weekend. They just needed us to do the breakfast shift, which we've done. So go on, get out of here.''

"Okay. I'll probably come here tonight anyway and lend a hand. I want to start to get to know some of the guys and get the place a little better organized.''

"Sounds good.''

The two women hugged. Gillian took off. Her mind still on Trace, Susannah went back inside to supervise the boys, and found them in the dining hall. Their work busing tables finished, their breakfasts eaten, they were doing Stupid Egg Tricks to the delight of the three part-time cooks and few remaining loggers, and to the detriment of several dozen eggs.

"Is GILLIAN TAYLOR here yet?" Cisco asked Trace quietly as he stepped into the dining hall office and closed the door behind him.

Trace finished typing the letter he'd been writing to Sam Farraday and did a save. "Been here and gone." Trace looked up from the computer screen. "Why?"

His expression unaccountably serious Cisco pushed back the edges of his Western-cut suit coat. "What did she seem like to you?"

Trace shrugged his broad shoulders noncommittally. "Nice. Efficient. Good-looking, if the waif look appeals to you." Trace sat back in his chair and pushed away from the desk. "Kind of sassy in the same way that Susannah and Patience and Callie and all women worth their salt are." He folded his hands behind his head, still studying his former nemesis and now friend carefully. "Why?"

Cisco let out a weary breath and scowled. "I wanted to talk to her," he said.

"What about?" Trace asked, understanding this was not a social call Cisco was intending to make.

Cisco's frown deepened. Abruptly, he looked older than his thirty years. "I went over that résumé she gave Susannah, and not everything on it checks out the way it should."

Despite Cisco's suspicions, Trace found it hard to connect the Gillian Taylor he'd met with anything criminal, particularly when she was so close to Susannah. Susannah did not have criminals for friends. Trace's glance narrowed as he inquired, "Did Max know this?"

"He told me not to worry." Cisco yanked at the string tie around his neck. "He said if Susannah trusted

Gillian, after they had worked together for nigh on ten years, that was good enough for him."

"But you're not satisfied," Trace concluded, moving back to his laptop computer.

Cisco folded his arms in front of him and lounged against the wall. "I think the discrepancies I found bear checking out. I've already done some digging, but to go any deeper I'm going to have to talk to her."

Trace thought it was ironic that Cisco would be making this particular complaint, since Max had rescued Cisco off the mean streets of Butte some fourteen years ago, when Cisco was just sixteen. To this day, Trace and his brother and sister were not sure exactly what kind of trouble Cisco had been in when Max found him, or even if he actually had been in trouble. They only knew that Cisco, who'd been something of a surly teenage delinquent at the time, had refused from the start to talk about his past. And that Max had also been mum about the subject, though mostly Max seemed just as in the dark about Cisco's background as the rest of them.

Despite all that, Max had taken Cisco Kidd—whose name bore, to Trace's thinking, anyway, a suspicious resemblance to the famed outlaw the San Francisco Kid—under his wing, straightened him out and eventually sent him to college and law school. In the process, Cisco had become not only Max's protégé and attorney, but also a highly regarded and trusted member of the McKendrick "family."

Trace found it odd, given the two men's close relationship, that Max had not mentioned Cisco in his will. Thus far, however, Cisco had not seemed to be at all concerned about that, either.

"You've met this Gillian Taylor, Trace. What's your opinion? Do you think I'm overreacting?" Cisco asked.

Trace shrugged and typed in the command Send. He stared at the screen, waiting for the flashing message that would tell him the letter had been sent. "I think you need to do what you feel you have to do."

Cisco frowned. Arms still folded in front of him, he moved away from the wall. "Then I'm going to have to follow my instincts and check her out," he said, opening the door to the dining hall once again.

"In the meantime, how about I get those boys off yours and Susannah's hands?" Cisco continued affably from the open door. "And give them a driving tour of the Silver Spur, starting here at the logging camp, then going over to the horse-breeding and cutting operation, and from there to the cattle ranch."

The prospect of spending more time with Susannah was a pleasant one. He wanted to get their relationship in order before the wedding, if at all possible. Cisco taking the boys off their hands for a while, would give them the time and space to do so. "It's okay with me," Trace said.

"What's okay with you?" Susannah asked, coming up behind Cisco.

Briefly, Trace explained.

The boys, overhearing their names, crowded into the tiny office to join in the discussion. "As hard as we all worked this morning, we deserve a break!" Scott said.

"Yeah! A ride in Cisco's Jeep sounds fun!" eight-year-old Mickey enthused.

"As long as we get to go fishing later this afternoon, like you promised, I'm in," Nate agreed, pushing his glasses up on the bridge of his nose.

"Me, too. Can we go, Dad? Can we?" Jason asked, bending down to tie his sneaker.

"After all, there's no time like the present to enjoy today," Scott drawled with a look in his mom's direction, as the boys waited simultaneously and impatiently for permission.

Trace looked at Susannah. To his relief, it was easy to see she hadn't the heart to deny them, either. "All right, but only on the stipulation that you boys behave. No fighting and no shenanigans of any kind," she declared, pausing to look all four of them in the eye. "Promise us?"

Promise us, Trace thought. He liked the sound of that...and the vision of the two of them parenting the boys together...

"We promise," the boys told Susannah in unison.

"I'll have them back to the lake house by lunchtime," Cisco said.

Susannah smiled, her expression a mixture of pleasure and relief. "Thanks, Cisco," she said gently.

The guys trooped out.

Susannah and Trace faced each other. Suddenly, it felt a little awkward, to them both. Trace decided to put her at ease. Although there was a part of him that very much would've liked to, he wasn't going to make a pass at her the second they were alone. The physical side of their relationship could wait until they had some of the other details of their union worked out, he told himself practically. But before he could do even that,

Trace knew, he had to finish what he had started this morning.

He stood, grabbing his suit coat and shrugged it on. "I've got to call my attorney about the Farraday deal." He paused a moment, aware once again that the terms of Max's will demanded the two of them stick to each other like glue. "It'd be better if I could make the call at home," he said, hoping she would agree to leave the dining hall after an almost five-hour stint.

Was it his imagination or did she seem to deflate a little at his request?

"No problem," Susannah said softly, turning away as she reached for her briefcase and purse. "I've got some work to do, too."

29:12

"YOUR SOFTWARE is out-of-date." Trace came up behind Susannah a long while later in a drift of brisk, masculine cologne. Palms flat on the kitchen table, he leaned over her. As he continued to invade her space in a completely maddening, utterly natural way, he told her, "You wouldn't have to keep scrolling from screen to screen if you had a program that allowed you to view and input data on several screens simultaneously."

Aware they were far too close for comfort, Susannah slipped out from underneath his flexed arm. "I know." As she slipped past him, she lost her footing for a second and her nose brushed the solid curve of his bicep.

"But?" Trace reached out and steadied her, with his hand on her upper arm, as if it were the most natural thing in the world.

Susannah inhaled sharply and stepped back, away from him, not stopping until she collided with the counter behind her. "It takes time to shop for software, install it and learn to use it."

Trace had his sleeves rolled up, his tie undone. Nevertheless, opposite him, in tailored pale yellow slacks and a matching sleeveless summer sweater, she felt almost underdressed.

"Not that long," Trace disagreed, his ocean blue eyes lasering in on hers with vexing practicality.

Susannah turned away from him and looked out the window at the sunshine shimmering off the deep blue surface of the lake. "Maybe not for a highly computer-literate person like you, Trace, but for someone like me who has just recently started to use computers, it is a big deal. Besides, I promised Max and Gillian that I would have the new menus from the dining hall worked out, the budget set and the supplies ordered by summer's end, and I've really got my work cut out for me if I want to meet that deadline, and I do."

Trace moved behind her, and looked out at the lake, too. "What do you have left to do?" He ran his palms over her shoulders, down her arms.

Susannah swung around to face him. "I have to finish going through the satisfaction surveys and request forms the loggers filled out for me this morning. From there, I need to decide how much variety is necessary at each meal. In other words, do I want one entrée or two or three."

Trace nodded, looking very serious. "How will you determine that?"

"The survey results," Susannah explained, smiling tremulously. "If everyone has requested chicken-fried steak, then I'll know it's safe to serve that and only that. If, on the other hand, two-thirds of the men have stated they absolutely loath chicken-fried steak, and the other third can't live without it at least once a week, then I'll know I have to serve it frequently as an alternate, instead of a primary entrée. Our goal is to make everyone reasonably happy, because as Max used to say, 'A well-fed logger is a happy logger. Ain't no one gonna work their best with a stomach full of somethin' he dislikes.'"

"That's true. We get more compliments and complaints about food than anything else at my camp, too." Trace paused and stepped back. "Once you've input all that into your computer, what next?"

"Then I have to make up a month of menus. Search out the recipes and adjust the components accordingly. Give them to Gillian, because she is, after all, the one who is going to be running the camp dining hall on a daily basis. If we're in budget, we'll figure out the supplies that need to be ordered, and do that. Once she's all set, and my consulting work is done, I'll return to work on my cookbook series."

Trace blinked in surprise. "You've already started on it?"

"I've been working on it off and on for the last seventeen years. I don't want to write just one volume. I want to do a ten-book series on the food of the West, including the history of each dish wherever possible, and suggestions on entertaining. I'll have more success if I can release the books all at once, as a set, rather than in piecemeal fashion."

"How many books have you finished so far?"

"Two. I'm still testing recipes in my spare time on the third."

"How long do you think it'll take you to finish?"

Susannah shrugged, wondering if it was her imagination, or was the kitchen a little smaller than she had originally thought? "Maybe a year or two, if I can hire a secretary and work on it full-time."

Trace paused, taking that in. Susannah saw the respect in his deep blue eyes, and knew it was because of the depth of her ambition, which in this one case, matched his own. The only difference, she supposed, was that she was able to keep her life in better balance while still going about the process of achieving her goals. Whereas Trace had to go at everything full-tilt, including her.

"In that case, new software is going to be a must," Trace said, glancing back at her computer.

Susannah sighed and tucked the bobbed ends of her hair behind her ears. "I'll get to that when I can, but it's not the first priority on my list." The first priority was trying to straighten out this situation with Trace so she could meet what she realized now was her commitment to him regarding their son, and still emerge from the effort with her heart intact. "And speaking of business, how did your call to your attorney go?" She knew there had been several after that.

"Fine." Trace gave her a satisfied smile, adding, "It took some doing, but I finally got Sam Farraday to agree to at least meet with me later this evening."

They were to be married tomorrow. Their personal lives were in what could only be called crisis. And he was still scheduling business meetings right and left,

Susannah thought with a sharp stab of disappointment.

Reminding herself it was essential for her emotional well-being to not go into this with any unrealistic expectations, where Trace and his complete devotion to business were concerned, Susannah forced herself to maintain a carefree demeanor as she smiled. "No rest for the weary, is there?" she commented dryly.

Trance slanted her an unreadable glance. "It would appear not."

An abrupt silence fell between them. Trace kept his eyes on hers. A veil of intimacy began to descend around them. Susannah pushed it away as her eyes dropped to her watch. She noted that Cisco and the boys had been gone for nearly two hours. Trace had been doing business for most of that. It was just as she thought. Some things didn't change. They could have spent this time together, maybe worked a few more things out. He'd had to tend to business first, last and always.

She swallowed around the knot of hurt gathering in her throat. "The boys should be returning soon." Sensing he wanted her to look into his eyes, she studied the loosened knot of his tie instead.

"I know they will." His hands on her shoulders, Trace edged closer. He looked impatient again, desirous. "And I'm sorry my business took so long, but this is something that had to be worked out—"

"I know."

"—*immediately* if we're to get married tomorrow, as planned."

Susannah was not so sure she agreed with that.

"But now that that's taken care of, before the boys get here, Susannah, I want to—"

Trace's words, the intimacy of the moment, were cut off as their four boys came tromping into the kitchen, Cisco on their heels. "See!" eight-year-old Mickey drawled with all the subtlety of a town crier. "I told you they'd be together."

"No surprise there," Scott said, rolling his eyes in exasperation and elbowing Nate in the ribs.

Nate elbowed Scott back. "I know what you mean," Nate murmured congenially, sizing up Susannah and Trace from behind the lenses of his glasses. "They can't seem to take their eyes off each other."

"Hey, Cisco. Does this mean they're gonna fall in love again?" Jason demanded, smoothing his cowlick with the back of his hand.

Cisco shrugged as he studied Susannah and Trace in equal measure. "It's what Max wanted," Cisco said.

But Susannah knew she did not want to be with Trace for that reason alone, because it was what Max had wanted, and she warned herself to be even more cautious.

The phone rang. Jason grabbed it off the wall, listened a moment. "Dad, it's for you," he reported. "Your office."

Again? Susannah thought, more than a little annoyed.

Trace did not look surprised. "I'll take it in the den."

Cisco consulted his watch. "I need to be going, too. I have to go check on Cody and Callie and Patience and Josh."

Reminded that Cisco was doing triple duty, carrying out the terms of Max's will, Susannah walked Cisco to the door. She paused in the portal, basking in the late-morning sunshine. "Thanks for taking the boys this morning. It gave me a chance to get a lot of work done."

"No problem. They're great kids. I enjoyed it."

No sooner had Cisco left than Jason came down the stairs, carrying a wadded-up T-shirt in his hand. "Susannah, do you know anything about getting stains out of shirts?" Jason asked.

Susannah smiled. When it came to running a household and mothering teenage boys, she was really in her element. "Quite a lot, as it happens," she told him warmly. "What have you got there?"

Jason held up a Hootie and The Blowfish 1996 concert T-shirt for her examination. "It's ketchup and when Dad washed it, it didn't come out. He said I should pitch it in the rag bag and not worry about it because I've got plenty of other shirts."

"But you like this one," Susannah guessed, wishing all of life's problems were this easy to solve.

"Yeah. And I'll never find another one like it, 'cause I already tried, so... do you think you can help me?"

Susannah figured this was the easiest problem to come her way in days. "We can give it a shot." She laced a maternal arm around his shoulders. "Where do you keep the laundry supplies?"

TRACE HEARD Jason's corny jokes and Susannah's laughter long before he hung up the phone. It brought a smile to his face. How long, he wondered, had it been since a woman's laughter had filled his home and his heart? Too long, he knew.

Mickey slipped into the den and hovered close to Trace's desk. Hand on his chin, he reported, "The guys say we're gonna go fly-fishing this afternoon."

Trace nodded. "That was the deal if you helped out in the dining hall this morning," he agreed, wondering what was up.

"There's just one problem with that," Mickey confessed gravely, edging a little closer. "I don't know how to go fishing. I've never been."

"So you probably want some instruction?"

Mickey nodded swiftly. Then apparently thinking better of it, he paused, saying politely, "Unless you're too busy."

Trace smiled. It felt good to be needed for something other than business, for a change. These days, more often than not, his two boys felt they didn't need him for anything anymore. "I've got time," Trace said with a smile. He stood and circled his desk.

Mickey fell into step beside him. As usual, half of his T-shirt was tucked into the waistband of his shorts, the other half was falling out. "Can you teach me how to throw the thing over my head?"

"You mean cast a fly?"

"Yeah," Mickey asked, his freckled face lighting up anxiously. "Can you?"

"Sure." Trace headed for the storage room adjacent to the garage, where all the recreational gear was kept. "But we'll have to go outside to practice. We can't exactly do that in the house."

Trace swiftly found a rod and reel similar to the one his two sons had learned on, and took Mickey out on the front lawn. Half an hour later, Trace noted with satisfaction, Mickey was remarkably proficient, for a beginner.

SUSANNAH FOLLOWED the trail of exultant male voices and walked outside to see what was going on. "So this is where everyone disappeared," she said, surveying Trace and their four boys, all in various stages of practicing their fly-casting.

Jason put down his rod and reel and hurried over to see the damp shirt in her hand. "Did it come out?" he demanded.

She held up the concert T-shirt for him to examine. "No, not yet. But there's one more trick we can try, if you're game."

Jason stared at his T-shirt as if it were a long-lost friend, then shrugged. "It's not like we have anything to lose at this point," he told her.

Together, they went back inside, Susannah explaining all the while, "The bad news is, the stain appears to be set in the fabric. The good news is, the stain is on the plain white part of the T-shirt."

Jason studied the array of laundry products on the table. "So we can bleach it?"

"Not all of it, 'cause if we did that it might mess up the color blocking on the rest of your shirt." Like a science teacher explaining the ins and outs of an experiment, Susannah continued, "Since the stain is on the white part, we can make up a solution of chlorine bleach and cold water, knot up the stained part, like this, and very carefully dip the stain into the bleach-and-water solution. Of course, we've got to be careful not to get any bleach on our clothes or in our face or eyes or anything."

Jason nodded formally. "Gotcha."

"You want to try it?"

He drew in a jerky breath and stuffed his hands into the pockets of his shorts. "How 'bout I just watch you, since this is my first time out with this kind of stuff?"

"Okay. Here goes." She dipped the small area of stained fabric into the solution and held it there. They waited for the results with bated breath. "Hey," Jason said after about three excruciatingly long minutes had passed. "The stain isn't red anymore. It's pink!"

"Yep. It sure is."

Two more minutes passed. "Now it's light pink!"

And then another. "It's white."

Not wanting anything to go wrong at this late stage, Susannah carefully transferred the shirt and soaking bowl to the laundry room sink. She cautiously disposed of the bleach-and-water solution, being careful not to splash, then rinsed the formerly stained fabric. "Now do we put it in the dryer?" Jason asked.

Susannah shook her head, correcting, "We wash it again first. But don't worry about that. I'll do it."

Jason reached forward impulsively and gave her a hug. "Thanks, Susannah. You're a lifesaver."

"I quite agree."

Susannah looked up to see Trace standing in the doorway. He nodded in the direction of the backyard. "The guys are still practicing their casting out there on the lawn if you want to join them," he told Jason.

"Yep, I do. Look, Dad! Susannah got the ketchup stain out of my T-shirt." He darted off to join the other guys, banging the door shut behind him.

Acutely aware of the way Trace was studying her, Susannah put Jason's T-shirt in the washer, along with a load of white towels.

Arms folded in front of him, Trace lounged in the doorway. Though he still had on his suit pants and dress shoes, as if he expected to be called to attend a business meeting at any moment, he had taken off his tie and rolled up his sleeves past the elbows. A wealth of crisp curling dark brown hair and suntanned skin was visible in the open neck of his shirt.

"Jason thinks you're a miracle worker."

Susannah flushed self-consciously. She wished she didn't want Trace to admire her, but she did. "Mickey thinks the same of you."

The full impact of his ocean blue gaze was focused on her face. "Seems both our kids have missed having a parent of the opposite sex," he said softly.

She knew it was true. More, she had missed having a man in her life. She had missed Trace...

"You're great with them," she told him softly, meaning it.

He acknowledged her compliment with his eyes. "So are you," he replied softly.

The moment drew out. He began to reach for her. She felt herself moving nearer, too.

"Dad!" Nate came racing in, Mickey fast on his heels. They banged the door after them, the noise forcing Susannah and Trace apart like a shot.

"Will you show Scott how to make his own lure?" Nate demanded.

"Yeah," Mickey added importantly. "He wants to know, but he doesn't want to ask 'cause he doesn't want to put you to any trouble if you're busy."

Trace smiled. "It's no trouble." He turned to Susannah with a shrug, "Duty calls."

Susannah turned on the washer, then went out on the front lawn to watch. As she watched him tirelessly instruct all four boys simultaneously, she was touched by Trace's patience and gentleness. She knew she had done him a great disservice, not telling him about Scott when their son was born.

She realized she could never give back to Trace what she had taken from him. Nor could she re-create those years. But there was something she could do, she thought determinedly. Something she should have done a long time ago. And the sooner the better.

Chapter Seven

"It's not fair!" Jason stormed as the two families gathered en masse in the manicured backyard.

"We always get to go alone," Nate said.

"How come we suddenly need a chaperon?" Mickey asked, looking a little clueless, too.

Trace frowned as he helped the boys gather up the fishing gear and prepare it for transport to the stream. "After the mess you made with the water balloons last night," he said heavily, kneeling next to a well-used rod and reel, "I would think that would be evident."

"So we goofed up." Scott defended the group candidly as he carefully restored order to a vintage wooden tackle box. "Now is our chance to show you how responsible we really are."

Though no one had asked her opinion on the matter, Susannah felt obliged to add her two cents to the discussion. She stepped into the center of the group. "I don't know about this idea of the boys going off alone, Trace. Scott and Mickey have never been fishing. They don't know the Silver Spur." There was so much that could happen!

"But we do," Nate protested quietly as he secured his own fishing pole and gave Susannah an imploring look. "And we promise you, we'll behave." When she still hesitated, his expression turned even more imploring. "Please. After all the hard work we did this morning at the dining hall, I think we've earned the chance to have a little fun."

As he joined forces with Susannah in the center of the group, Trace draped his arm around Susannah's shoulders. "You're talking about going to the stream?" Trace asked his two sons.

Jason nodded. "The one where Nate and I catch all the trout."

"It's a tributary to the Silver River, Susannah, and it's only four feet deep right now," Nate added with scholarly precision, "'cause it's been a while since it rained."

"They'll be safe there, I promise," Trace said. Turning slightly, he studied Susannah's upturned face. "You'd probably feel better if you could see it, though, wouldn't you?"

She nodded.

"Grab your gear and your sunscreen, guys, while Susannah and I pack the lunch hampers. We'll all head out there. If Susannah approves, you'll be on your own for the afternoon. If not, she and I will hang around with you."

The boys dashed off to comply. Trace turned to her. "I can also leave them with a cell phone. That way, if there's any problem, they can call and we can get out there immediately."

"You really think it'll be okay?" Susannah followed Trace inside, to the kitchen.

Trace nodded as they began to put together a lunch for the boys. "But just to make sure, I have an idea," he said.

"WRITTEN CONTRACTS?" Scott echoed incredulously fifteen harried minutes later.

"To go fishing!" Nate blinked behind his glasses.

"We've never had to do that before," Jason complained, smoothing his cowlick.

"What's a contract?" Mickey asked as he knelt to retie his sneaker.

"A contract is an agreement signed by both parties, spelling out what they will or will not do," Trace said patiently as he sat all four boys down at the kitchen table, while Susannah finished loading up the picnic hamper with sandwiches, chips, cookies and cold drinks. "I figured it would be a good idea to go over the rules in writing before Susannah and I turn you loose. So, here's the deal." Trace paused to hand out copies of the "contract" he had quickly prepared on his laptop computer and portable printer, then continued explaining sternly. "There is to be no fighting of any kind. All fishing equipment is to be shared equally. All questions about fishing or the ranch are to be answered politely. If anyone needs help, they need to ask for it nicely. We expect you all back home by five this afternoon. Any and all catch will be cleaned and prepared for dinner at that time."

"Cool!" Jason said, starting to sign the document without reading it.

"Sounds good to me." Mickey followed suit.

Nate read on, frowning as he studied the fine print at the bottom. "Wait a minute, it says here we'll be grounded, according to parent-house rules, if we don't live up to our end of the bargain,'' he observed.

"Right,'' Trace said.

"Fair enough, for an afternoon of freedom and recreation,'' Scott said.

Looking happier than Susannah could recall seeing him in quite a while, Scott signed with a flourish. The other three boys soon did the same.

Their meeting concluded, their lunch packed, Susannah and Trace walked with the boys through the woods to the stream. After about twenty minutes, they reached the famed fishing hole. "Oh, Trace, it's gorgeous here,'' Susannah said, looking at the sparkling stream beneath the canopy of trees. Toward one end of the clearing, there was a wide sandbar that spread across the center. The water in the channels on either side of it was only a half a foot or so deep, which made crossing to the grassy bank on the other side very easy, Susannah noted as Nate and Jason rolled up their pants legs and waded right in.

"One of the reasons the boys love it so, I think,'' Trace said.

She nodded, looking around. There was practically no current to the stream. Mickey and Scott were both excellent swimmers. Scott had also taken Red Cross lifesaving classes the summer before.

Trace continued to study her while she studied the site. "Think they'll be safe enough?'' he asked as the boys began setting up their lines, Trace's sons offering both help and advice to hers.

"Yes,'' Susannah said as the last of her anxiety fled. Maybe this was exactly what the boys needed. Certainly it would help blend them into a single family.

While Susannah watched, Trace finished helping the boys set up their rods and reels, and spread out a couple of blankets upon which to have their lunch. It was clear there was a broad spirit of cooperation among them. Watching, Susannah was very pleased.

Trace handed over the cell phone to Scott and Nate. "Since you two are the oldest, I'm leaving this with you."

"We'll be okay," Scott promised Trace in a man-to-man way.

"Yeah, Dad," Nate added. "We'll be fine."

Because they were clearly not needed, and were in fact mostly in the way, Trace and Susannah said goodbye to the boys and headed back to the lake house through the woods.

They fell into step beside each other, with Susannah wondering if this was how it was going to be.

"Want to explain that expression on your face?" Trace remarked almost too casually after a while.

Susannah started. She hadn't realized her anxiety was that evident. "What expression?" she asked, to buy herself some time.

"The same one you've had since you came downstairs and found the boys signing contracts."

Susannah shrugged a shoulder as she ducked to avoid a hanging branch. "I was just wondering if you have to run absolutely everything like a business deal." Her fingertips grazed a leafy green tree.

Trace moved to the side to let her pass first when the path narrowed. His hand resting lightly, proprietorially, on her waist, he followed her through. "It works better that way, if you take a logical systematic approach." Their shoulders brushed as the path widened enough to allow them to walk side by side again. "The real question is, what are we going to do with ourselves during this unexpected reprieve?" Trace asked. His steps slowed slightly as they entered the backyard. "We've got five hours ahead of us."

Susannah knew what she wanted to do, although she wanted it to be a surprise. "If you have no objection, I'd like to take our first thirty-minute break apart," she told him politely, keeping her intentions to herself. "I have an errand to run."

Disappointment flared briefly in Trace's deep blue eyes as he came to a halt. "You want to meet me back here?" he asked after a moment, his casualness as studied as her own.

Her heart pounding at his nearness, Susannah shook her head, aware that even on their romp through the woods, Trace had remained dressed in his suit pants and dress shirt, though he had long ago discarded his tie altogether. "No. The boys might show up and I don't want them to walk in on us unexpectedly while we're talking." She consulted her watch and decided after careful consideration that she had time. Her eyes lifted to his once again. "I'll meet you at the hunting lodge in thirty-minutes."

TRACE WALKED into the hunting lodge and stared at his surroundings. It was just as he remembered, nearly half a century old and constructed of rough-hewn logs in a rectangular one-story design, with a high, vaulted roof. A large room, plenty of windows and a flagstone fireplace dominated the front part of the lodge. Toward one end of the open area was a cozy kitchen, furnished with a heavy-duty black Aga stove that Max had imported from England as a wedding present for Susannah, and a large silver refrigerator that was also a wedding gift, from Susannah's mother. Toward the other end was a conversation area, with an overstuffed pine-green sofa and two wing chairs. There was a shelf filled with books on forestry. A captain's desk. A bedroom beyond with a big split-rail-framed double bed where they'd once slept, and a bathroom with a huge old-fashioned claw-footed tub that Trace had always planned but never quite got around to proving, was more than big enough for two. Beside that was another bedroom that had served mostly as a storage room, for it had no furniture.

As Trace roamed the small, cozy lodge, he thought back over the past seventeen years. He hadn't spent much time at the lodge since the morning Susannah left. Being there had simply been too painful. He'd thought it better to move on, so shortly after she left him, he'd moved his business headquarters to northern Montana, and set up a home there. Then, he hadn't felt he was running from the past or the present. Now, in retrospect, he knew he had been. Because what he'd felt for Susannah had never really been over. He had been fooling himself, thinking it had been.

A noise sounded behind him.

Susannah came in, looking breathless and windblown, her bobbed sable hair in sexy disarray. Her arms were full of old photo albums and several small boxes.

His pulse picking up a notch, Trace quirked a curious eyebrow.

"I can't give you back the time with Scott that I took away from you, Trace." Susannah came toward him in a drift of perfume. "But I can fill you in on what's happened in the years since." She put her cargo down on the coffee table. Taking his hand, she led him toward the sofa, her expression that of a gift giver on Christmas Day. "It's all here," she told him softly as she sat down beside him like the friends they had once been. "Baby albums. School photos, report cards, soccer trophies, everything."

She opened a box of loose photos—some of which bore the scars of the quake—and spread them over the coffee table. Moments of his eldest son's life lay before him. Trace suddenly felt angry that he'd been cheated and deprived of nearly sixteen years of his son's life, but he quickly reined in his errant emotions. Susannah didn't have to share these pictures with him, he thought. Two wrongs would never make a right and he wanted to start fixing all that had been wrong with them. To do that he would have to put this hurt behind him, which—he hated to admit—would be no easy task....

Trace focused on one rather crumpled picture of Susannah and her family visiting Disneyland. Scott was eight, Mickey little more than a baby. The man next to her had a friendly, freckled face and strawberry-blond hair. "This is your husband?" Trace asked.

Susannah nodded. "I met him shortly after I arrived in California. My father had a small character part in a movie out there. Drew was a writer who worked for the studio. He had been brought in to punch up the dialogue for one of the stars. My father introduced us and we began seeing each other."

"You got involved awfully fast."

Susannah nodded, a distant look in her eyes. "I was scared and I was pregnant. He wanted to take care of me and my baby." She paused to draw a halting breath. "And he had the kind of job where he could work at home most of the time."

Trace studied the picture of Drew. He couldn't say why exactly, but it was a relief to him that Drew looked like a decent sort of guy. "Did you love him?"

Susannah frowned as if she had been expecting that question. "He loved Scott and Mickey fiercely. He was an excellent father to the boys."

"You're not answering my question."

"He was a good father and husband and, yes, I cared a great deal for him." Her shoulders stiffening slightly beneath the clinging cotton fabric of her sweater, Susannah stood. As she moved to draw one of the blinds so the early-afternoon sun would not be in their faces, she replied, "Not in the way you mean, not in the passionate way you and I were in love when we first got married. But I had feelings for Drew from the very first, and our friendship grew into a deeper, steady, more familial kind of love," she continued, choosing her words carefully as she came back to sit opposite him, in the far corner of the sofa. "Our home was a tranquil one. No real highs or lows. Just a comforting haven from the outside world."

Trace tore his eyes from the pictures long enough to slant her an inquisitive glance. "Did you ever feel like you were missing something?"

As she considered that, Susannah's eyes darkened to a deep sable brown.

"Sometimes." She brought her espadrille-clad feet to the sofa cushion, her knees to her chest, and laced both her hands around her upraised knees. "What about you? What was your second marriage like?"

"Pretty much the same as yours, I gather." Trace continued to go through the pictures, one by one, enjoying the visual history they made.

"Calm and peaceful?"

Trace nodded, knowing it was no exaggeration to say it had been. "Natalie's father had been a self-made man and CEO, so she knew from the get-go what her life with me would be like and she accepted that. If I missed dinner or had to go out of town for weeks on end, as sometimes happened, I never had to worry about her complaining."

"She must've been very understanding."

Almost too understanding, Trace thought. To the point where he had sometimes felt as if he was almost an unnecessary and somehow incidental part of Natalie's life. "She was a very competent woman. And she was a great mother to the boys."

"It shows. Jason and Nate are great kids."

"So are Scott and Mickey."

Silence fell between them. Trace turned back to the baby albums. His mood veered between the deeply sentimental, to yearning, to melancholy.

Susannah seemed to be feeling the same torrent of emotions. After a moment, she asked, "Would it have made a difference? If I had told you I was pregnant before I left, would anything have changed?"

It was an honest question. It deserved an honest answer. His gaze holding hers, Trace replied, "If you're asking me would I have worked shorter hours or not been away as much, the reverse is probably true. I was trying so hard to make a home for us, to prove I was a man. Knowing we had a child on the way probably would only have intensified my drive at that time." He had been, after all, only twenty-one.

"I see." Susannah stood. She was unable to completely mask her hurt.

Trace felt his own hurt feelings come quickly to the flashpoint. "What's done is done," he said gruffly, vaulting to his feet after her. "All we can do is go on from here."

"But can we?" Susannah whirled to face him. "Or are we just making things worse by getting involved again—even to this point?"

Trace saw the tears in her eyes, the hurt on her face, and knew he had to do something—anything—to get past the no-win situation they had been in all these years.

Acting purely on instinct, he wrapped his arms around her and took her into his arms, testing the waters cautiously. "We have to do something for Scott," he told her firmly.

Susannah splayed her hands across his chest, her fingertips grazing the hard muscles of his chest. A pulse beat wildly in her throat. She stepped back slightly. Because he refused to let go of her, she remained caged in his arms. "This isn't for Scott," she said, beginning to tremble.

"*I know.*" Trace murmured softly as he lowered his mouth to hers. He had things to make up to her, just as she had things to make right to him, now, he could think of no better way to ease either of their pain. No better way for him to win back control of their lives. "It's for us."

Their lips met in a firestorm of need. Years of pent-up passion spilled into their kiss. Hours of yearning intensified everything they felt.

Before she knew it, Susannah was standing on tiptoe, pressing all of her against all of him. With a low moan of satisfaction, Trace threaded one hand through her hair. His other hand splayed across her spine, urging her closer yet, so their kiss could deepen. And with his every move came the need to be so much closer.

She trembled as his hand slipped beneath the hem of her sweater and moved upward, skimming over her breasts. Her response to his touch, instantaneous. Susannah heard him groan deep in his chest.

Seconds later, he was dancing her backward, through the doorway, to the bed. Excitement pounded through her as he unzipped her slacks and pushed them down her thighs, still kissing her all the while. The linen pooled around her ankles. One hand pressed against her lower spine, the other moving downward from her navel, he slipped his palms inside the elastic of her bikini panties, caressed her warmly. Intimately. Knowingly. She wouldn't have thought it possible, but she jerked against him, in shock, then shuddered again, as the liquid heat inside her began to implode. She whimpered, low in her throat, as he made her tremble, again and again and again. Then his hands danced up her sides, over her ribs. He dispensed with the clasp of her bra and gently cupped the weight of her breasts with both palms.

He let the kiss come to a slow, languorous halt. One that spoke of volumes of control. His eyes were darker, sexier, than she had ever seen them.

"I want you," he whispered, already lowering her to the bed. "I want you now. Here." He slipped between her thighs. "This way."

Susannah's breath came in quick, shallow spurts. She knew they were rushing things. She didn't care. She helped him with the zipper on his slacks, surged up against him, every inch of her wanting every inch of him. "I want you, too," she whispered back throatily. "So much."

Trace stroked her face as the hot, heavy length of him strained against her open thigh. Shifting lower so he was positioned exactly where he should be, he took her back into his arms. She was trembling with a fierce, unquenchable ache. Even as he lowered his mouth to kiss her again, even as their kisses melted one into another, as she strained against him, her body moving in undulations, she knew this wouldn't solve everything. It wouldn't make her closer to him. It wouldn't erase the past nor guarantee the serenity of their future. But it would do something toward sating this fierce, unquenchable ache. And for the moment, she thought as his hands lifted her and he surged into her, powerfully, lovingly, that was enough. It had to be.

SUSANNAH LAY tangled in the sheets, the right side of her face resting against the pillow. She might have her back to Trace, but there was no disguising her reaction to what had just passed between them. Her breath was still coming in shallow spurts. Her body was still humming with the aftershocks of their lovemaking. And all the emotions, every ounce of feeling she had suppressed over the years apart, was now coming to the fore. She knew making love now, while they still had so much unresolved between them, when they might never resolve everything between them, hadn't been the smartest action for them to take. On the other hand, they'd had to do something with all that emotion simmering between them. Who was it that had said, make love, not war...?

"What are you thinking?" Trace stretched out beside her. He was also lying on his side.

Susannah sighed and rolled to face him. Like it or not, there were some things they had to confront. And discuss. "That I should have told you I was pregnant," Susannah confessed softly, fixing her gaze on the sexy mat of golden hair furring his sinewy chest.

"Why didn't you?" Trace caught her fingers and brought them to his mouth, where he suckled them gently.

Susannah melted a little at the new wave of desire surging through her. She let her head rest against his chest as he wrapped his arms around her. "I wanted to, but I didn't think you wanted me or a baby in your life at that point. And I didn't want our child to grow up feeling the way my mother inadvertently made me feel when I was growing up."

"And how was that?" Trace stroked her hair with gentle motions of his palm.

Susannah cringed, recalling, "Like an unmet obligation. Something to feel remorseful and guilty about."

Trace paused, his grip on her loosening. "Your mother did that to you?"

Susannah pushed herself to a sitting position. "She didn't mean to react that way. I realize that in retrospect," she told Trace as she propped a row of plump comfortable pillows between the split-rail headboard and her spine. "But at the time, all I knew was that her work as a surgeon came first, always. It didn't matter if she had promised she would attend my school play or piano recital." Settled comfortably back against the pillows, Susannah dragged the sheet up over her breasts. "If something came up at the hospital, a patient took a turn for the worse, she skipped whatever was going on in my life and my father's, and stayed to take care of the patient."

Listening intently, Trace sat up, too.

"When she would eventually get home," Susannah continued, "which was almost always hours after dinner, she would be physically and emotionally exhausted. Most of the time, she had already eaten and didn't even remember what she had missed."

Trace's eyes turned a very stormy blue. "But you did," he guessed softly.

Susannah nodded, the memories she had strove so hard to forget coming back to haunt her. "And so did my father," she explained as she linked hands with Trace. "He never let her go unchastised when it came to broken promises, and that went double for promises she had made to me. The end result was, they quarreled constantly."

Trace's fingers tightened over hers. "You never told me any of this."

Susannah shrugged, embarrassed. "They had been divorced for three years by the time we met and married. My father had given up teaching drama in high school and moved to Los Angeles to pursue an acting career in film. I was trying to put it all behind me and build a new, more satisfying life for myself."

"Only to find yourself married to and at the emotional mercy of yet another workaholic," Trace concluded heavily, his own regret apparent.

Susannah sighed, letting him know with a look that she wished she had not made that mistake, either. "That pretty much sums it up," she admitted reluctantly.

"You should have said something to me then," Trace scolded her gently, wrapping an arm around her shoulders and holding her even closer.

Susannah studied the pattern of sunlight falling through the trees outside and through the windows. She was stunned at how easy it had been to make love with Trace again, and even more amazed by how right it felt. "I didn't know how to even begin to articulate my needs to you without turning into a nagging shrew. Besides, all the complaining my father did hadn't helped my parents' situation any. All it did was make them more bitterly isolated from each other, and consequently, me. My mother's ambition was constant. It wasn't going to change then, no matter what he said, and to this day it still hasn't," she said emphatically. "My father, on the other hand, needed more of a homebody for a mate. Once he stopped expecting my mother to magically conform to his needs, and he found that in someone else, he became very content, too."

"So your parents are now happy?"

"Deliriously so."

"Did your mother ever remarry?"

"No. She decided long ago that she was the kind of work-driven person who needed to stay single."

"So, at the time you left me, you thought I had the same woefully ineffective potential to be a mate and parent as your mother."

"Yes, although, having seen you with your sons, I now know how much I misjudged you, Trace. Unlike my mother, you're a wonderful parent to your boys."

Trace frowned, admitting, "More so now than when Natalie was alive. Sad to say, back then, I left quite a bit of the parenting to her. More than was fair, I see in retrospect."

"But you've made up for it."

"Yes. I have."

If only I could make it up to you and Scott, Trace thought. For he knew Susannah was not a cruel person. If she had not told him about their son, it was because he hadn't met her needs as a husband, lover and friend.

Once again, he had failed someone close to him by not being sensitive enough. The question was, how to keep that from happening again. He couldn't read her mind. She had admitted, when push came to shove, that she had trouble articulating her needs. Which in turn left only one solution.

He turned to her, knowing there was a risk in his proposal, more in not making one. "We can't go into this second marriage as naively as we went into our first," he told her firmly.

Susannah pushed the silky length of her hair from her face. "I'll agree with you there," she said wryly.

Which left them only one solution, Trace decided swiftly. "To protect ourselves from similar hurt and unhappiness, to make this new arrangement of ours work on every level, we need a more businesslike approach to our relationship.''

At the word *businesslike,* Susannah blanched. Her fingers tightened on the sheet. ''Actually, Trace—'' She looked oddly desperate, even as Trace struggled to put her at ease. ''I— I don't think we should even discuss this,'' she sputtered.

Thinking like hers was precisely what had gotten them into trouble before, Trace was certain. ''Well, I do.'' He disagreed, his mood altering from blazing passion to tenderness to frustration with lightning speed. ''We need a marriage contract,'' he said.

Chapter Eight

Susannah stared at Trace. Whether Max had meant for this to happen or not, somewhere in the last twenty-three hours she had become a challenge to Trace that he was determined to surmount by whatever means necessary. The stakes, in the desperate situation they suddenly found themselves in, were high. Their future happiness depended on them being able to make this relationship work in a way it never had before. She was no longer able to deny her desire for him. The realization of just how vulnerable she was shook her to the core.

Susannah leaned back against the headboard, staring at him incredulously. She clutched the sheet tightly to her chest. "You're kidding, right?"

"I never kid around when it comes to contracts." Trace leaned away from her as he rummaged in the nightstand for a notepad and pen. Finding both, he let the sheet drift past his waist and sat back against the headboard. "We can get started on it right away. Spelling out the dos and don'ts of our relationship. That way," he continued with startling efficiency, "we won't have any misunderstandings about our expectations of each other.''

Abruptly, Susannah felt as if she was part of one of his business deals, and not a particularly necessary part, at that. Gritting her teeth, she grabbed the bedspread, wrapped it around her, toga-style, and got out of bed. "This is not a good idea," she announced as she rummage around for her clothes.

"Of course it is," Trace disagreed politely. "What better way is there for us to avoid the pitfalls we suffered before? Now, where do you want to start?" he asked, his blond eyebrows lifting emphatically.

Susannah ducked into the bathroom to put on her bra and panties. "How about with lovemaking?" Susannah suggested sarcastically.

There was a thoughtful silence from the other room. "Okay," Trace said agreeably a moment later. "What seems reasonable to you?"

Susannah slipped her sweater on over her head and padded back into the bedroom. "You're serious, aren't you?" She paused to tug on her slacks.

"What seems reasonable to you?" Trace persisted, seemingly irritated that she would not be as cooperative in stating her needs and expectations as he planned to be. "Three, four times a week?" He kept his eyes on her face. "Every day?" His smile widened recklessly as he lobbied for the latter.

Susannah found her shoes, and reaching into her purse, pulled a brush through her hopelessly mussed hair. "Or would you prefer to go in the other direction as far as guarantees go, say... once or twice a week?" Trace continued.

Finished, Susannah dropped the brush onto the distressed surface of the rough-hewn bureau and pivoted to face Trace. Hands braced on either side of her, she returned his probing gaze with one of her own. "What happens if we decide on twice, and then end up making love six times that week? Do we subtract it from the next three weeks, until we're on schedule again, or charge ourselves a penalty?"

Trace shrugged his broad shoulders. Putting aside the notepad and pen, leaving the sheet on the bed, he walked naked to her side. "Making love above what we decide on as the norm seems more like bonus material to me."

"It would."

He took her into his arms. "You're angry."

Susannah splayed her hands across his chest and pushed away. "Heck, yes, I'm angry! How can you even suggest such a thing?" she demanded as heat started in her cheeks and swept across her face in both directions.

Trace stepped back slightly, a perplexed expression on his handsome face. For once not bothering to mask his obvious confusion, he asked incredulously, "How can you expect us to get by without one?"

Susannah rolled her eyes and, aware she was still barefoot, began to hunt for her shoes. "This is impossible."

Trace scooped up his clothes from the pile on the floor. "It doesn't have to be," he said as he pulled on his boxers and slacks.

Susannah swept into the other room. "You cannot run our marriage with the same single-mindedness that you run your company."

"Not without your cooperation, I can't." Trace followed, buttoning his starched white dress shirt.

Deciding it might be wise if they remade the bed, Susannah hurried back into the other room. "I agreed to marry you and stay married to you because of Scott. But that is as far as I am willing to go when it comes to making myself part of any deal." She picked up the top sheet and tossed it over the bed.

Trace grasped the opposite corners of the sheet and tugged until they were lying straight. He tucked in the corners, hospital-style, and reached for the bedspread. "You're just angry because you found out you are not over me, Susannah, any more than I'm over you," he said as he threw the bedspread over the sheet.

"How do you figure that?" Susannah asked, aware telltale color was still rioting across her face.

"By the way you just made love to me." Trace tossed one pillow to her, and threw another on the bed. Finished with his side, he circled the bed to take her in his arms once again. He studied her with a hungry expression. "We owe it to each other to try again," he said firmly.

He felt warm and hard against her. Too warm. Susannah levered herself away from him. "I don't see that anything has really changed." Once again, she marched into the living room.

"Then help me make things change." Trace followed her lazily, picking up his wing-tip shoes as he went. He sank down on the sofa and put on his shoes. "You can start by spelling out for me just what it is you expect and want in a husband, and I'll do the same. Maybe if we exchange priority lists, we'll have more luck pleasing each other.'' Giving her no chance to get a word in edgewise, he decreed bluntly, ''In the meantime, I think we should tell the boys at supper that we have decided to make our marriage a real one in every respect, starting in twenty-four hours.''

Beginning to feel completely overwhelmed, Susannah shook her head. ''It's too soon.'' Trace was simply stepping in, making all the decisions, taking charge again. And she was not going to allow it.

She folded her arms in front of her. ''I want to stick to our original plan. Marry according to the will, then see how things go.''

''Meaning?'' Trace rolled lazily to his feet.

Susannah resisted the urge to back up as he came toward her. ''Meaning, we shouldn't tell the boys our marriage is going to be a real one unless we are sure our relationship is going to last,'' she said seriously. The part of her that was always looking out for her children, and herself, and keeping one eye on the future, would not be completely banished, no matter how inexpedient Trace found her worry. ''Until then,'' she continued sternly, ''it'll have to be one step, one day at a time, with establishing a lasting friendship our first and primary goal.''

The disappointment reflected in his deep blue eyes briefly took her aback. Aware it was not her purpose to hurt him any more than she had already hurt him, she sighed, amending, ''If we can be lovers and make our relationship work, great. If not, for Scott's sake, we still have to maintain our friendship.''

Trace studied her. "All right," he said finally, giving in to her practically stated options. "We'll do it your way, for now."

Susannah could see he hadn't given up on his goal of ultimately having her as his wife in every sense. The question was, did he love her, or just want her in his life again? She knew he didn't like to fail at anything any more than she did. Unlike her, he was compulsive about going back to fix anything flawed that he had left in his wake, until it, too, was as perfect as he wanted.

Was that the situation with their marriage? she wondered. Was he simply trying to right what he had once failed to achieve? And if so, how long would his interest in her and their marriage last?

24:01

"YOU'RE A CHEF, right, as well as a consultant?" Nate asked Susannah an hour later. Having already cleaned the fish, Trace and the boys had all headed upstairs for showers. Nate, the speediest and most efficient of the boys, was the first to come back downstairs, where he had promptly joined her in the kitchen.

Susannah smiled at his question and gestured for him to have a seat. "I sure am. Do you want to help me with the menu for dinner?"

"Sure." Nate poured himself a glass of milk then joined her at the table, where she was busy filleting the fish into serving-size portions. "What'd you have in mind?"

As Susannah studied Nate, she thought about how much he looked like Trace. "We'll have the trout you all caught, of course. What else do you think everyone would like?''

Nate shrugged. "I don't know."

Finished cutting up the fish, Susannah dropped the pieces into a shallow dish and covered them with milk. "I was thinking about corn on the cob, slaw." She knew they had the ingredients for both in the pantry and fridge.

Nate watched as she mixed flour, salt and pepper. "Do you know how to make scalloped potatoes?"

Susannah smiled. She put aside the flour mixture, and sliced several lemons. "I sure do."

"From scratch?"

"From scratch." Susannah chopped parsley, too.

Nate continued to watch, looking fascinated as Susannah added peanut oil to a large cast-iron skillet. "What about apple fritters?"

"Those, too."

Nate rested his elbow on the table. A dreamy expression came into his eyes as he reminisced, "My mom used to make apple fritters, sprinkled with powdered sugar. It was one of her specialties and they were so good." Nate made a comical face. "Dad tried to make 'em once, but they were a disaster. All gummy and chewy and icky."

"He probably forgot an ingredient or didn't get the oil temperature right before he fried them." Susannah studied Nate's wistful expression. She knew what it was like to be a kid and not have your needs met. "Do you know what recipe your mom used?" she asked.

"No." Nate gulped the rest of his milk, then wiped his mouth with the back of his hand. "She had her recipes written down somewhere. I don't know what happened to them." He frowned, some of the light going out of his eyes. "Does this mean you can't do it?"

"Nope. It means it's just going to be a little harder, and I'm going to need your help." Susannah brought cabbage and freshly shucked corn out of the fridge. "You said something yesterday that makes me think you know a lot about computers. Is that true?"

Nate nodded. "I can work my way around the Internet."

"What I want you to do for me isn't nearly as hard. I've got a great data base on my computer that draws recipes from all sorts of cookbooks. So, if we type in fritters, and then type in apples, we'll get a mix of different recipes. If you'll take my laptop and hook it up to a printer, I'll get the rest of dinner going, and then we can do some detective work on the fritters."

Nate bounded out of his seat. "You really mean it?"

"Sure. If you don't mind taste-testing a variety of apple-fritter recipes."

Nate grinned from ear to ear. "It sounds like a tough job, but I think I can handle it."

Susannah was elbow-deep in potatoes, when the heavy tread of footsteps sounded on the stairs. Trace strode into the kitchen, looking incredibly handsome, in navy blue Dockers and a short-sleeve madras sport shirt. It was the first time she had seen him in anything other than an ultraconservative business suit and tie since she'd been back. Susannah felt a thrill sweep through her. Was she responsible for his time-out from work? Or would it have happened anyway? The clothes looked brand-new, or at the very least, barely worn...

Knowing they only had a few minutes alone—if that much—and that she needed to talk to him alone, without Nate or any of the other boys overhearing, Susannah dried her hands on a dish towel, gripped Trace's forearm and tugged him into the pantry.

"I don't know what's happening, but I like it," he drawled.

Susannah placed her index finger against his lips. "I have something to tell you," she whispered. And she didn't know how he was going to feel about it. She hoped that what she was about to say wouldn't rock the boat. "Nate asked me if I could make apple fritters for dinner, the way his mom used to make them. He's hunting up recipes for me now."

Trace shook his head, recollecting humorously, "The ones I made were pretty bad."

Susannah breathed a sigh of relief. "Then you don't mind?"

He shook his head as his hands tightened around her waist, sending ribbons of warmth up and down her spine. "I think it's great. I want my boys to remember Natalie every bit as much as I want them to get to know you."

"Well, it's good there's room for both of us in their lives, 'cause I think it's important that our kids keep their other parents close to their hearts, too," Susannah said.

"Agreed." When she moved to step past, Trace moved with her, smoothly barring her way. His blue eyes twinkled with mischief as he studied her. "Aren't you forgetting something?" he drawled in a low, sexy voice that intensified the shivers of awareness ghosting up and down her spine.

"What?"

"This," he said softly. Their lips met with lightning quickness and summer heat. Susannah was filled with wonder—that the attraction between them could be so powerful and intense. He made her want him, want this. He made her feel alive. And she hadn't felt any of those things, she thought, as she kissed him back fervently, for so damn long. Too long.

Trace knew he was taking advantage of the moment as he crowded her against the pantry wall and continued to kiss her with all the hot-blooded finesse he possessed. He didn't care. Susannah was back in his life again, he thought as his hands swept over her and he left a string of kisses down her jaw, before he once again returned to a slow, sensual exploration of her lips. With Max's help, she would stay. And, he thought, still kissing her madly, he would give her reason to never want to leave him again.

The sound of footsteps tromping down the stairs forced them apart. Susannah muttered her frustration at having gotten caught again. Trace muttered his frustration at having to stop.

Blushing fiercely, Susannah vaulted into action, shoving bags of potatoes and onions into his arms while she gathered up the powdered sugar and cinnamon. Together, they emerged from the pantry just as the boys marched in.

Susannah knew her hair was mussed, her lipstick gone. To her chagrin, it quickly became apparent that not only had their four boys noticed her disheveled appearance, they knew why she looked that way.

Mickey remarked with a cheeky grin. "They're at it again."

Jason nodded with exaggerated solemnness. "Can't keep their hands off each other."

Scott drawled, "Worse than teenagers, if you ask me."

"Found 'em!" Having missed the commotion, Nate came in waving a sheaf of papers.

"Found what?" Scott asked curiously.

"The fritter recipes," Nate announced.

"Susannah's making fritters?" Jason asked excitedly.

"For dessert," Nate confirmed happily as commotion swirled all around.

"Hey, Trace. Can I ask you something about business schools?" Scott said, pulling a chair up to the kitchen table.

"Sure." Trace sat opposite him, his attention focused solely on their son.

"Do you think it's worth it, going Ivy League?" Scott continued. "Or dollar for dollar, are state schools a better buy?"

"YOU'VE BEEN SMILING all evening," Trace said hours later as the two of them settled on the chain-hung porch swing overlooking the lake.

"What's not to smile about?" Susannah replied happily, tucking her hand in his. "Nate and Jason were deliriously happy to have the apple fritters they so fondly remember and very appreciative of my culinary efforts. Scott listened carefully to all you had to say this evening and is actually starting to think about his future. Mickey learned how to cast a fly rod and caught a fish. Add to that, the boys are not only all getting along and bonding well, they actually volunteered to do the dishes.'' It seemed miracles would never cease.

''It feels good, doesn't it?'' Trace stretched an arm along the back of the swing.

''What?'' Susannah moved into the warm cradle of his arm.

''The two of us coming together again, blending our two single-parent units into one family,'' Trace said.

''My boys have missed having a dad around.''

''Mine have missed having a mom.''

Which was yet another reason they should stay together, Susannah thought contentedly as Trace sifted the soft curling ends of her hair through his fingers. ''So, how is it that you turned out to love cooking so much?'' he asked softly, reminding her that she hadn't taken it up until well after they'd divorced.

Susannah sighed, knowing she had come to her career as a chef in a roundabout way. ''It's a long story.''

Trace moved the swing back and forth in a slow, soothing way. He shifted inexorably closer, tucking her into the curve of his arm. ''I'd like to hear it, anyway.''

Susannah leaned her head on Trace's shoulder, realizing all over again how much she enjoyed just being with him at quiet times like these. The problem was, they had never had enough of them. ''It all goes back to when I was a kid,'' she confided, ''and the fact my parents' work schedules were very different. Because my dad was a schoolteacher, he had all the holidays and summers off, whereas my mother's medical practice kept her working six and seven days a week, twelve to eighteen hours at a clip.'' Susannah shook her head, recalling, ''My dad used to get so upset when he would go to the trouble to make dinner and then my mom wouldn't show up to eat with us. My cooking the evening meal was a simple way to make peace. Somehow, it wasn't so bad that my mother missed dinner if my father hadn't been the one spending a couple of hours in the kitchen preparing it. So, as I was able, I gradually took over cooking dinner. It gave us a measure of peace, and eventually led to my habit of cooking whenever I was under stress, period."

"I seem to recall you doing a lot of baking in the early days of our marriage."

The proceeds of which, Susannah thought with fleeting irony, Trace had never been around to eat. "The reasons for that were twofold. One, I was frustrated at not being able to get a job in my chosen field, which was teaching home economics, since most of those classes were being systematically phased out of the schools, not expanded. Two, baking helped relieve the stress I felt at the way our marriage seemed to be falling apart day by day." And it had given her some sense of trying to be a good wife.

"When we divorced, did you teach then?"

"No. I still couldn't get a job. So, rather than get certified to teach something else like history or math, I picked up some work as a chef, and liked it so much I decided to make it my vocation instead. I did that for about ten years, working at several different restaurants and even a catering business, then finally entered the consulting field, and worked with restaurants on revamping their menus, largely because I liked the more flexible hours and the creativity that led to my current career as consultant slash cookbook author." Susannah paused, as she lifted her face to his.

"You love your work, don't you?" Trace observed. Susannah nodded, proud of all she had accomplished. "Very much. Cooking well is a real art."

"Your parents must be very proud of you."

"They are. Although initially my mother accused me of choosing a career in home economics precisely because she was so very bad at it." They laughed together, knowing beneath the facetious statement there was a grain of truth.

She paused, wondering suddenly if she knew everything about his past. "What about your parents?" she asked Trace curiously. "Your father was a surgeon, too. Did your mother ever mind his frequent absences?" That was a common complaint of doctors' families, she knew.

"No." Trace pressed a kiss on her forehead. "That was never a cause for tension in our house, it was just the way things were," he confided acceptingly. "Of course, since my mother was a nurse and had often worked on his surgical team both before and after their marriage, she understood full well the demands of his job at the time they married."

"Your life was just about perfect when your parents were alive, wasn't it?" Susannah guessed, knowing she would always envy him that.

Trace nodded as he caressed the soft inside of her wrist. This was familiar ground, as he had often talked to her about his family in general and his parents in particular when they were together, but it felt good to be covering it again, to be picking up where they'd left off. He had loved and admired his parents in the same way he had wanted to be loved and admired by his sons. "I know it sounds like a cliché, but life with my folks was like a Disney movie. Everyone was happy and safe and loved.''

Trace frowned, his own insecurity coming to the fore. ''After the earthquake, when Patience and Cody and I went to live with Uncle Max, things changed. Cody was always an unusually quiet kid, even at six, but he withdrew something fierce after Mom and Dad died. I thought then he just needed more time alone, to sort things out. Now I think maybe he needed just the opposite. But I was so busy tending to Patience, who was always a lot more vocal about her needs, that I didn't see it,'' he said sadly.

Susannah was sure Trace was being too hard on himself. ''You think you failed him?''

Regret flashed in Trace's blue eyes. ''Sometimes . . . when I see what a hermit he's become in recent years . . . I think so, yeah.''

''And maybe that would have happened, anyway,'' she said tranquilly as dusk fell and the crickets cranked up their chirping. ''If there's one thing I've learned, Trace, it's that there's no predicting in this life. Things happen. And when they do, we go on as best we can.''

''No do-overs?''

''Not in this life,'' Susannah affirmed. Much as they might want to, they simply couldn't turn back the hands of time. ''But that's not all bad,'' she continued softly, anticipation for the future—their future—racing through her as she held his eyes, ''as long as we learn from our mistakes.''

From the steady way Trace looked at her then, Susannah knew he wanted to kiss her again. Not to prove a point, not for revenge, or to seduce. But because he felt the connection between them, too. The connection that was growing with every second they spent together.

"So what next, in your view?" Trace asked huskily.

"We concentrate on doing better in the future," she told him in a low, serious tone. "Luckily for us, this setup Max engineered really seems to be working," Susannah reflected happily, thinking once again how well everything suddenly seemed to be going, despite the odds to the contrary.

"I'll second that," Trace murmured with obvious satisfaction as the boys trooped out to join them.

"Here you go. You're all set," Scott and Nate said, handing over a wicker picnic basket. "Don't worry about us. We older brothers'll hold down the fort at home," they vowed earnestly.

"And we younger brothers promise to behave," Jason and Mickey said in unison.

Susannah glanced at the faces of all four boys. Clearly, all five males were in cahoots about this, and had been for some time. "What's going on?" she demanded, pretending to be a lot more incensed than she really was about this latest surprise.

"You and I are going over to the hunting lodge for the evening," Trace informed her magnanimously.

Susannah blinked, struggling to determine what that meant. "On a date?" Was Trace getting romantic on her? And what exactly was in that picnic basket?

To her disappointment, Trace tensed in a very unchivalrous way. "Actually, I've got a business meeting," he said.

"With Sam Farraday," Susannah recalled reluctantly, something he had told her much earlier in the day, and she had promptly—purposefully—forgotten. *And because of the will, I have to go with you.*

"Why not hold the meeting here?" she asked Trace, surprised he wasn't wearing a suit again. At least then, she could busy herself spending time with the boys.

Trace shrugged. "The lodge is a lot closer to the main highway."

The lodge was also filled with all sorts of memories, Susannah thought, both good and bad. Plus, it was an ideal place to be alone and to make love, as they had passionately proved that very afternoon. Did Trace plan for them to put business first, and their relationship a distant second, as always? Or was this evening to be business only? she wondered, feeling a little crushed. Maybe, she thought uncertainly, despite evidence to the contrary, things weren't going so well, after all....

"It's okay, Mom, really it is. We'll be fine," Scott told Susannah, totally misreading the reason behind her visible apprehension. "We *want* you to go and have a good time," he insisted.

"Yeah, make a date of it," Jason suggested, already waving them off.

"We promise we won't wait up, if you decide to be late," Nate teased.

"Yeah." Mickey high-fived them both. "Go for it, Mom!"

Go for it.

Indeed.

Trace waited for her to decide. It was clear what he wanted to do, what they all wanted her to do. "I'm beginning to feel outnumbered," Susannah teased with a levity she didn't really feel.

Yet, the alternative—to show how incredibly vulnerable she was feeling at just the prospect of giving her heart to Trace all over again—was equally unthinkable. The will, the knowledge of his son, had given Trace enough of an edge over her already.

"As well you should," Trace agreed with a mock gravity that amused their rambunctious boys all the more. He stood and helped her to her feet. "Thanks, guys. As always, you can telephone me on the cellular phone if there are any problems."

"Will do," Jason promised.

Susannah and Trace headed toward his dark green Jeep.

He sent her several cautious glances but did not speak until they were well on their way. "You seem upset," Trace noted after a while as he picked up the Jeep's speed slightly.

Susannah folded her arms in front of her and looked at the trees whizzing by her window. That was the understatement of the century. "Should I be?" she queried coolly.

"Suppose you tell me," Trace drawled.

He really didn't know why she was so upset, Susannah thought incredulously. "I take it you think there shouldn't be a problem if we combine business and pleasure?" she guessed dryly. She was upset that the evening seemed slated mostly for business.

"Anything that gives us a chance to be alone that the boys will buy works for me."

But did it work for her? Susannah wondered emotionally. "Is that the only reason you want me along on this business meeting?" Susannah demanded. She tensed, reluctantly recalling how many evenings during their newlywed days she and Trace had planned just for themselves had ended up being geared toward his business dealings instead. It wasn't a practice she wanted to reinstate. "So we'll have a chance to be alone later, to make love again?" So he could cement the business of their getting back together, for Scott's sake, the same way he was cementing this business deal with Sam Farraday tonight? So he could, heaven forbid, talk her into signing some sort of marriage contract that spelled out their various duties and obligations in very unromantic detail?

Her life was turning into a nightmare of have-tos and I'm-too-busy-for-us all over again.

Trace shrugged, his assessment of the situation as matter-of-fact as his mood. "I figured it might help speed things up and cinch the deal with Farraday if you were along. You always were good at making people feel at ease," he commented genially, one hand circling the wheel, the other reaching over to squeeze her knee companionably. "And with Sam Farraday flip-flopping, ready to sell one minute, ready to call off the whole thing the next, I figured yours might be a reassuring presence."

"I see," Susannah said tightly, beginning to feel very much taken for granted. Worse, she had a premonition of many similar evenings ahead. Darn it all, anyway.

"Problem?" Trace said as he parked in front of the lodge and cut the engine.

Hell, yes, there was a problem. Susannah swiveled toward him furiously. "You might have gotten away with this in the past, Trace McKendrick," she warned, slamming out of the Jeep. "Not anymore."

Chapter Nine

"You can't use our relationship as a tool to help you get ahead in business, Trace," Susannah said as the two of them squared off in front of the Jeep. She'd known this wouldn't work from the outset. Why hadn't she listened to her gut feelings. Instead, she'd allowed herself to be seduced by their passion. "I want our second thirty-minute break apart, Trace. Now." She held out her palm, expecting him to give her the keys to his vehicle.

Instead, he withheld them stubbornly. "I have a commitment to Sam Farraday in fifteen minutes," he told her, as if that, and not their relationship, was the most important thing going.

She gave him an icy smile. "Then drive me over to the dining hall and drop me off there. You've got time to get there and back and still have five minutes to spare before Sam Farraday arrives. Meantime, it'll give me a chance to pick up my Suburban." And get hold of my skyrocketing temper, she thought defiantly.

Trace paused contemplatively. "You'll meet me at the lodge in thirty minutes?" he specified bluntly.

"Yes," Susannah replied impatiently. Max, darn his meddling soul, had given her no other choice.

The tense set of Trace's shoulders relaxed slightly. "We're going to talk about this, Susannah," he warned officiously, opening the passenger door for her.

In the meantime, business was first, as always, Susannah thought resentfully as she climbed back into the Jeep. They drove over to the dining hall in tense silence. Susannah sensed Trace's mind was already on the business ahead of him as she wordlessly slipped from the car and walked into the nearly empty hall. To her relief, only Gillian remained after the dinner shift.

"To what do I owe the honor of this visit?" Gillian asked mildly, her surprise at seeing Susannah evident as she rearranged the cafeteria-size bottles of condiments on the supply shelves at one end of the kitchen.

Susannah fumed as she rolled up the sleeves on her cerulean blue knit dress and pitched in. "Men!"

"One in particular, I presume."

Susannah jerked her head in the direction of Trace's departing Jeep, unable to recall when she had been so angry in recent years. "Needless to say," she complained hotly, "that ex-husband of mine hasn't changed one bit."

"Really?" Gillian grinned as she selected a place for the various kinds of steak sauce. "How so?"

"He can't do anything without it somehow relating to business."

"We're talking about his remarriage to you?"

"And about tonight," Susannah said hotly. "And our after-dinner date. At least what I first thought was supposed to be a date for just the two of us. Only now it turns out it's more of a business thing, with me playing hostess to a difficult negotiator from whom he is trying to purchase some prime Montana timberland." And that in turn had torn down the new bond building between them. She had hoped—thought—that the passage of time and the advent of his children had taught him to open up his life to more than just work. To learn to relax and enjoy his life, and those in it, if not every day then at least from time to time. They'd had such a wonderful afternoon, marred only by his desire for a marriage contract. The supper hour, spent together and surrounded by their sons, had been even better. She had loved the intimacy of sitting with him in the porch swing, rocking back and forth and talking quietly. Just as she loved making love with him. Only to discover his thoughts had not been focused on the two of them, after all. He had probably been secretly thinking about this business deal of his all day.

"You feel used, I take it?"

Susannah hated to admit it, but it was true. "Wouldn't you?" she asked Gillian, noting the wind was beginning to whip up outside. When she and Trace had been married, the only time she'd seen him in the evening was when he'd been doing business with a client and needed her along. She had felt like an ornament on his arm then; she felt like one now.

"I don't think that's the question here," Gillian said gently as she lined up ketchup bottles, one by one.

"Then what is?" Susannah snapped, her frustration and hurt momentarily getting the best of her.

Gillian smiled faintly. "Do you really want to walk away from the inheritance Max left you, not to mention Trace, and the chance to try again? I mean, from things you've said off and on over the years I've known you, I thought the abrupt end of your first marriage was one of the great regrets of your life.''

Susannah sighed heavily as she raked both hands through her hair. "It was.''

"So?'' Gillian waited.

"It isn't a question of what I want,'' Susannah countered wearily. If only it was!

"Oh, I think it is,'' Gillian disagreed, suddenly looking so much wiser than her years. "Take it from me. There are some things in life that can't be fixed, and there are some that can, Susannah. When it comes to your failed marriage with Trace, you still have time to salvage the relationship.''

I AM NOT DOING this for me, I am doing it for my children, Susannah told herself firmly as she parked her Suburban in front of the hunting lodge, some twenty-nine and a half minutes after she and Trace had parted company. If she adhered to the terms of Max's will, she could provide her two boys with a beautiful home—in this case, the hunting lodge—and the kind of financial security only a major publishing deal, like the kind Max was offering, could bring.

If providing for her sons meant she had to swallow her pride in the meantime, Susannah schooled herself fiercely as she pushed from her Suburban and walked past the white Jaguar in the driveway and Trace's Jeep, then so be it.

Putting on the smile she reserved for the most difficult clients, she stepped inside the hunting lodge, and was hit with her second surprise of the night.

Trace was seated on the sofa, a lovely auburn-haired woman some ten years Susannah's junior, beside him.

They had a sheaf of papers spread across both their laps. So engrossed were they in the business before them, they didn't even notice she had come in. Watching them together, Susannah felt a sharp stab of jealousy, one that was only partially related to Trace's utter and complete devotion to his business.

"I don't know, Trace." The beautiful woman beside him toyed with the lapel on her striking black-and-white business suit. "I keep thinking maybe I should go into partnership with someone like you, instead of sell my land and timber outright."

Trace frowned, his displeasure with that suggestion evident. "I'm not taking on any partners, Sam. I made that clear at the outset of our dealings." Turning, Trace noticed Susannah had come in. He stood gracefully and made introductions to his guest. "Sam, Susannah Hart. Susannah, this is Sam Farraday."

"Short for Samantha," the lovely auburn-haired woman added with a smile as she stood. "Congratulations on your wedding. I'm very excited about attending."

"Thank you." Susannah shook Sam's hand. "It's a pleasure to meet you," she told Sam. To Trace, she said as she backed up slightly, "I'm sorry. I didn't mean to interrupt."

"No problem. Sam and I were about finished." Trace turned to Sam and gave her an uncompromising look. "Twenty-four hours, Sam. One way or another. If you don't want to sell, fine. I'll look for something else."

"I understand. I'll try to come to a decision before tomorrow morning."

Trace showed Sam out. They talked a few minutes more on the front porch of the lodge, then Sam got in her car and sped off.

Trace returned to Susannah. "I wasn't sure you were coming back."

I wasn't, either, she thought. Susannah shrugged, trying not to make too much of it, for fear she'd only be disappointed again. "It seemed like the right thing to do."

Trace glanced at his watch, then began to pick up his copies of the sale contract. "I'm glad you made it within the allotted time," he said as he slid the documents into a folder and back into his briefcase. "I was beginning to worry."

"That we would be disqualified from the will?" Susannah asked casually.

"That something had happened to you," he specified. "That you'd had a flat or something between here and the dining hall." He inclined his head toward the way the wind was blowing through the trees. "It looks like it might rain."

"I've driven in rain before, Trace, plenty of times," Susannah retorted crisply. "And as you can see, I didn't have a flat tire."

He studied her as if wondering what tack to take. "As you can see, my business was concluded as quickly as I promised."

Or was it? Susannah wondered, recalling that Sam Farraday had not seemed at all done with Trace. "Is she interested in you?" Susannah hadn't meant to blurt that out, but now that she had . . .

Trace waved aside the question with an impatient gesture. "I'm not interested in her. Why?" He regarded Susannah steadily, looking just the tiniest bit pleased. "Are you jealous?"

Yes, embarrassingly enough, Susannah thought, she was, even though she could tell by the slightly annoyed look in Trace's eyes that she had no reason to be. Experiencing a strong sense of relief, she continued curiously, "Is that why you wanted me here with you tonight, and talked up our wedding even as you ruled out any idea of a partnership with her, to discourage Sam Farraday?" If so, it made sense.

Trace shrugged, not above admitting casually, "I thought it might be a way to let her know there was no hope things were going to change, in that regard, or any other."

"I see," Susannah said coolly, beginning to feel used again.

Trace gave her a look. *Do you?* his expression said. *I wonder.* "Sam Farraday is without a doubt the most indecisive person I have ever known. I'm at my wit's end, trying to wrap up this deal with her."

"Then why persist, aside from the fact you want her timber?"

"Because the bottom line is, she has to sell. She's living in Denver now. She can't care for her family timber operation from there, although she's tried mightily for the last four years or so. Nor is she willing to give up her dual positions with the Denver Symphony and the University of Colorado—she's a violinist."

"So one way or another, she has to sell eventually," Susannah concluded, beginning to get the picture.

Trace nodded. "Or see what her family spent years building fall completely to ruin."

Susannah paused thoughtfully, considering another option. "If a partnership is the only way she can assuage her conscience and still sell the land to you—" Why not?

"I'm not interested in a partnership with her or anyone else, Susannah," Trace said flatly as he moved around the lodge, drawing the drapes against the encroaching darkness.

How well she knew that, Susannah thought.

"But enough about the Farraday deal." He started toward her as the first sounds of rain pelted against the roof. "Whatever happens with it, happens. I'm more concerned about you and me," he confessed, a glint of happiness coming into his blue eyes. "I'm glad you came back tonight."

Oddly, now that she was here with him again, so was she.

Gillian had been right. Susannah knew she would regret it if she didn't try everything possible to make this work, to at least find a way to be friends with Trace. Maybe the way to do that, she mused, was to concentrate on what they had in common, rather than their differences. "Have you spoken to the kids?" she asked as he gently clasped her wrist.

Trace shook his head as he kissed her palm. "I suppose it is time for a call," he agreed. Releasing her reluctantly, he reached for the portable phone, handed it to her then watched as she dialed.

"Everything okay there?" Susannah asked her son Scott when he answered on the first ring. She wished she had a sweater. With the advent of the wind and the absence of the sun, the evening had taken on a definite chill.

"Not to worry, Mom," Scott reported cheerfully. "Everything's fine. We just made some popcorn. We're all watching *Indiana Jones and Raiders of the Lost Ark.* I'd forgotten what a cool movie it is. I'm glad Nate reminded me. Oh, and don't worry about the windows," he continued, automatically ticking off everything he knew she'd want to know. "We made sure they were all closed when it started to rain. You and Trace just take care of his business with that client and enjoy yourselves."

Susannah could hear from the background noises that the boys were engrossed in the movie and enjoying themselves. Any guilt she felt at not being with them that evening faded. "Call if you need anything," she urged.

"We will. Promise. Gotta get back to the movie." The phone clicked a split second later as Scott hung up.

"All's quiet on the home front?" Trace asked as Susannah shut off the phone.

Susannah shivered and nodded, feeling both amazed and pleased that her evening with Trace had been saved, after all. "In fact, they want us to take our time getting back," she admitted, grinning at the unexpected but welcome reprieve from the twenty-four-hour-a-day duties of motherhood.

Trace grinned, too, as he knelt to build a fire in the grate. "Get the feeling our kids are matchmaking?"

"And then some," Susannah conceded ruefully. As were Gillian, Uncle Max and Cisco.

"Does it bother you?" Trace lit the fire. He headed to the kitchen and returned with a bucket of champagne on ice.

"I admit there's a part of me that doesn't completely trust this newfound cooperation of theirs," Susannah admitted, watching as Trace uncorked the bottle. "Twenty-four hours ago, they were ready to cheerfully demolish one another with water balloons. Now they're going fishing and doing the dishes together."

"I see your point. It was a fast turnaround. Then again—" Trace poured two glasses of champagne then tugged her onto the sofa to watch the flames "—getting in and out of trouble together gave them something in common, as did busing tables at the dining hall this morning." He paused to hand her a glass of champagne then tucked her into the circle of his arm.

Susannah sighed as she sipped the sparkling wine. "I know it's unwise to look a gift horse in the mouth, but Scott has never been this well-behaved for this long."

Trace sipped his own champagne, as outside, the wind and rain picked up slightly in intensity. Susannah could tell by the look on Trace's face that he was lamenting all the years he had missed, years that could never be made up. "You're saying he gets in trouble a lot?"

"Mischief, and yes, he does." Susannah released a sigh of regret, sorry she hadn't been able to do more about that. For boys his age, she sensed it sometimes took a man to get the point across, which was something Trace understood. "He's always out to explore something or test his limits in some way, so finding him suddenly so completely and energetically cooperative is just a little...unsettling.''

''Maybe being in Montana is testing him,'' Trace said finally.

''That could be.'' Or maybe he and the other boys just had something else up their sleeves, Susannah thought. Usually, when the boys were this good for this long, it meant they were desirous of or up to something. With effort, Susannah shook off her uneasiness. The excessively good behaviour of all four boys the last twenty-four hours could be their way of making up for their misbehavior the evening before, she thought.

''It is very different here from California,'' she continued pensively, giving Trace's theory due consideration.

''Although I understand his need to prove his mettle in absolutely every way possible,'' Trace continued casually, revealing more of himself than he had perhaps intended to, as he stroked her shoulder thoughtfully. ''That's a trait inherent to all McKendricks.''

Susannah settled more snugly in the curve of Trace's body as they both propped up their feet on the coffee table. ''You and Scott are a lot alike. I noticed that at dinner tonight when he was talking to you about the merits of various business schools.'' She tilted her face to his, adding, ''Which, by the way, is something he has never done. Usually when I try to talk to him about college, he refuses to engage in a real discussion.''

''That makes me doubly glad he came to me, then,'' Trace said with paternal pride. ''If he is going to try to get into investment banking, he needs to get into a top school from the outset.''

Susannah studied Trace with a racing heart. "You'll help him?" For Scott, it would be a dream come true. For her, too.

"Of course," Trace said with a warm, companionable smile. "In fact, I was thinking he might want to come to work for me for the rest of the summer, as sort of a junior administrative aide. I could teach him all about the lumber business that way, from the bottom up."

That sounded great. Susannah knew there was a hitch. "Will Nate mind?" she asked worriedly. "I mean, I had the impression that Nate was already helping you out in that capacity." No matter what happened, she didn't want Trace's children, or her own, to feel slighted.

"Trust me. I have plenty for them both to do. And no, Nate won't mind, as I usually have half a dozen interns working for me every summer and following me around, so he's used to sharing me with others. But enough about my business. It's time to talk about yours," he announced magnanimously, putting aside their empty glasses and helping her to her feet.

"What are you talking about?"

He urged softly, "Come and take a look." Still smiling mysteriously, he led her into the bedroom, past the split-rail double bed where they had made love earlier in the day. There, on the desk, was a laptop computer. Perplexed, Susannah fingered the tag on the carrying case. "This has my name on it," she said. But it wasn't hers.

"And completely updated software which will make your consulting work a lot easier and more efficient," Trace supplied.

Stunned, Susannah swung around to face him. This was a gift? From Trace? When had he had time to do this? How had he managed? she wondered incredulously, as busy as he had been. "It has occurred to me that, before, I didn't give enough attention to your needs," he told her seriously, taking her all the way into his arms once again. He gently smoothed the hair from her face. "Now, I'm going to try." He cupped a hand beneath her chin and slanted his mouth over hers. His kiss was hot and sweet and completely overwhelming in its tenderness. For a moment forgetting her earlier anger at him for dragging business into their evening together, Susannah wreathed her arms around his neck and met him more than halfway. Engulfed by a wave of passion long held at bay, she let his hands stroke down her back, up her sides, to her breasts. She let him deepen the kiss to thrilling heights. Marriage to Trace had never been like this, she thought. Trace had never been like this. But she loved the changes time had wrought, and the new single-mindedness he had brought to their relationship...

Trace hadn't intended for the kiss to get so hot so fast. He hadn't intended to make love to her that afternoon, either. But he had. To the short-shrifting of their getting to know each other again as intimately as they needed to know each other, for them to have even a prayer of making this relationship of theirs work.

With difficulty, he ended the kiss, telling himself all the while this could be continued later.

As he released her, Susannah spied a large gift-wrapped box on the bedroom bureau. The slightly bedazzled look leaving her sable eyes, her soft lips opened in an O of surprise. Delight sparkling in her eyes, she nudged Trace's shoulder. ''More presents?''

To Susannah's dismay, Trace frowned and looked just as stunned to see the gift as she was. ''Not from me,'' he admitted reluctantly. He glanced at her. ''I take it this isn't from you, either?''

''No.''

Curious, Trace crossed the room to retrieve the gift box and brought it back to the bed. The tag read For Susannah and Trace. Brimming with an interest as lively as his own, Susannah sat down opposite Trace and undid the ribbon. Trace lifted the lid. Nestled inside the tissue were seven round-trip tickets to the South Pacific, hotel reservations, a signed contract for a college-age tour guide and companion for the kids and a note from Max. They read it together.

Dear Susannah and Trace,

Most times, honeymoons are taken without the kids. But in your case, I figured you would be wanting all four of your boys—and the companion hired to watch over them—close at hand. So for once, both of you forget about your work and enjoy the time off in tropical paradise. Remember, I've always believed in miracles and I'm a'rooting for you.

Love,
Max

''I wonder how this got here,'' Susannah murmured, delighted at the fairy-tale quality her life had recently taken on.

"Cisco, probably," Trace said, a crooked smile tugging at the corners of his lips.

"Max thought of everything."

"Yes, he did." Trace released a sigh of deep satisfaction. With the tip of his finger, he directed her gaze to the typed itinerary. "Notice the date on the tickets?"

Susannah's eyebrows drew together as she noted, "The departure date is the day after the wedding." She looked up at Trace. "He must've had a lot of faith that we would reconcile quickly," she murmured, amazed.

Traced admitted confidently, "He knows I don't like to waste time. Like him, I prefer to get things wrapped up as soon as possible. And that goes double for my personal life."

A chill went through Susannah. Trace had not meant to hurt her. He was just being honest. Nevertheless, once again, she felt more like a challenge Trace had decided to meet than a bride-to-be. Her feelings in turmoil, she propelled herself gracefully to her feet and moved to the window. Simultaneously, Trace's cell phone rang. Trace strode into the other room to answer it.

"I'VE MADE UP my mind," Sam Farraday said at the other end of a very staticky line. "I'm selling, to you, ASAP, according to the terms previously set."

"Great," Trace told her. He wanted this over.

"I want to sign the papers as soon as possible," Sam continued on the other end.

"No problem," Trace assured her. He turned to see what Susannah was doing. She was standing at the window, looking out at the gusting wind and rain.

Though the night outside was dark and gloomy, thanks to the fire he had built earlier, the inside of the lodge was filled with a warmth and light not unlike the kind Susannah brought into his life.

"How about tomorrow night?" Trace abruptly became aware of what Sam Farraday was saying. "After the ceremony, of course," Sam continued.

She was talking about doing business during the wedding. "During the reception?" Trace repeated, not bothering to mask his astonishment. He had known from the outset that Sam Farraday was remarkably self-involved, but the thought of doing business—any business—during his wedding was carrying things a little too far.

"It works for me," Sam said. "And you know I'm only going to be in Montana for a couple days."

But it doesn't work for me or Susannah, Trace thought. Firmly but kindly he told Sam just as Susannah walked into the room, "The reception is an inappropriate time."

"Then just before the ceremony?" Sam persisted.

Trace looked over at Susannah. Her long sleeves were pushed halfway up her forearms. Her hair was soft and mussed. Her bare feet were tucked into sandals. She wore little makeup, no jewelry, yet she had never looked sexier than she did at that moment. It was all he could do to keep his mind on the deal, and if it weren't for the fact that he had worked on it for months now, he would be tempted to forget it altogether. "Before the wedding is likely to be a little crazy, too," Trace told Sam distractedly.

"Then when?" Sam persisted, beginning to sound a little annoyed he wasn't being more cooperative now that he finally had the deal he'd wanted so long.

Trace knew it was now or never. The Farraday property would secure the fiscal success of his business for years to come. With four boys and a wife to take care of now, he couldn't turn away from the long-term financial security this deal offered. "How about nine tomorrow morning?" he suggested after a moment. That way he could get it all wrapped up before the wedding and honeymoon. "We can meet here at the ranch."

"Sounds good," Sam retorted happily on the other end. "I'll see you then."

Trace hung up to find Susannah glaring at him furiously. "I can't believe you," she fumed, not giving him a chance to get a word in edgewise. "You're doing a business deal tomorrow morning?"

Some things never changed, Trace thought, equally piqued. At the mere mention of his business, Susannah flew off the handle.

"Our wedding isn't until four in the afternoon," he told her calmly, unable to understand why she looked as if he had just sold her down the river.

"You are incredible," Susannah said, flabbergasted. "You haven't changed a bit."

Trace had an idea what she was thinking. He reassured her with a great deal more patience than he felt, "My signing a few papers will not interfere with our being together."

"Don't you get it?" she retorted exasperatedly. "It already has."

His own temper skyrocketing, Trace regarded her stoically. He had already explained why this deal was important to him. He couldn't understand her attitude, unless she was still locked into some old behavior patterns, too.

He regarded her steadily. She was making him feel as though he had failed her again, and though in the past she had often been right about that, this time he knew he didn't deserve it. "I'd have thought having a career of your own would've taught you the importance of honoring your commitments," he told her coolly, wanting to get their mutual priorities set from the get-go.

"Exactly." Susannah paced the room grimly as hot, angry color swept into her face. "Only in my case, I know what comes first. Family, Trace. Not another acquisition. When will it ever be enough?" Her brown eyes glittered with hurt. "For heaven's sake, you're almost as rich as Uncle Max!"

Trace knew it would never be enough until he stopped feeling as if the rug could be pulled out from under him at any second. Seeing to finances was only step one of his master plan for his family. "When you calm down, you will realize this is no big deal," he told her calmly, knowing this was not going to change. The sooner the Farraday deal was closed, the sooner he could concentrate fully on rebuilding his relationship with Susannah. That would be good for all of them.

"You're wrong, Trace. This is a very big deal." She yanked open the door and rushed headlong out into the pouring rain. In the distance, lightning flashed.

Determined to stop her from walking out on him once again, Trace was hard on her heels. "Where are you going?'' he demanded, annoyed with her foolhardiness.

"I don't know!" Susannah shouted, whirling away from him. "I don't care!"

Her impetuous words hit him like a sucker punch in the gut. Worse, they were familiar. He grasped her by the shoulders and spun her around to face him. They had only been outside a few minutes and their clothes were soaked to their skin. "You can't drive in this storm." He regarded her with ambivalence. *It wasn't safe.*

"Watch me," she sputtered, wrenching herself free of his detaining hold.

The wind whipped up with a mighty gust as thunder roared overhead, but it was nothing, Trace thought furiously, compared to the storm going on inside of him. He grabbed her wrist and wrested the car keys from her hand. Slipping an arm beneath her knees, he scooped her into his arms and carried her onto the porch of the hunting lodge. He set her down promptly, then backed her up against the rough exterior side of the lodge. His expression stern, he braced an arm on either side of her.

Leaning in close, he pressed a light, fleeting kiss across her lips. Another across her cheek, her temple, her forehead. "You're not walking out on me, Susannah. Not again."

SUSANNAH TREMBLED at the sizzling contact of his lips against her skin. She had wanted Trace to come after her before, to prove that he loved her and did not want a divorce after only three months of marriage. Then, she hadn't felt one-tenth of what she felt for him now, maybe because the intervening years, combined with seeing and being with him again, had made her realize just how precious and rare what they had shared really was.

To the right of them, the rain continued to come down in torrential sheets. To the left of them, warmth and light spilled from the open doorway. Safety was just steps away, Susannah thought, trembling. Heartbreak, too. She knew she couldn't bear to fall in love with Trace again, only to lose him to his work, and like it or not, she was falling in love with him. His devotion to his work was interfering with their life even now. She had no reassurance it wouldn't continue to be that way.

She curved her hands around the flexed muscles in his arms. It was late. She was tired, and alone with him like this, feeling far too vulnerable. She hitched in a breath. "I can't go back to living the way we did before, Trace." Her low voice vibrated in the soft silence of the evening. *I can't go back to constantly being disappointed.*

He threaded his hands through the damp strands of her hair as lightning zigzagged in the distance, and thunder roared. "I'm not asking you to do that," he soothed, stroking down the length of her hair with gentle, mesmerizing motions.

If only that were true, Susannah thought on a soft, sad sigh. "Aren't you?" she asked, trembling all the more at what she felt. He had the potential to hurt her as no one ever had or ever would.

"No," he said roughly, hauling her into his arms and tightening his grip on her just enough to make her heartbeat unsteady. "I'm not."

His lips slanted over hers in a fierce implacable way that left her no choice but to respond. And respond she did, with all her heart and soul. Twining her arms around his neck, she opened her mouth to his, accepting the searing, deliberate thrust and parry of his tongue. As his hands slid over her back, she arched her body closer yet, reveling in the hard feel of his body pressed against hers.

She gave a little cry as he swept her into his arms and carried her inside the lodge. He shut the door with his foot, and continued toward the bedroom. His eyes locked with hers, he set her down beside the bed. Together they undressed. Together, they lay down in the cool linen sheets. His mouth came down on hers, touched briefly, then moved to her nape, where it traced sensual patterns of his own design. And dropped lower, to the uppermost curves of her breasts. "Trace," Susannah moaned.

"What?" He caught her nipple in his mouth and tugged gently.

"I want you. Now," Susannah whispered fiercely as his hands cupped her breasts and nimbly worked her nipples to crowns.

She felt his arousal, pressing against her, even as he kissed her again and again, until her insides were hot and melting and she whimpered against him.

He moved so they were lying on their sides. "Like this?" he whispered as his palms slid lower. He cupped a hand around the nest of sable curls. The other flattened against the small of her spine. "or like this?" Eyes locked on hers, he stroked her dewy softness, moving up, in.

"Yes," she whispered, watching his eyes gleam with distinctly male satisfaction as she followed his lead and caressed him passionately, too. "Like this," she whispered as they kissed again, first slowly and lingeringly, then hotly, rapaciously. Until there was no doubting they needed each other, they needed this. Not to just survive, but to thrive. Until she surged up against him, every inch of her, wanting every inch of him.

And yet even when the passion had quieted, when their bodies were sated, and they lay twined together, their hearts still beating as one, she knew nothing was settled. He still wanted things his way. When faced with turmoil, her gut reaction was to close down her feelings and head in the opposite direction. Certainly, that method of self-protection worked to minimize the risk of being hurt. But it did nothing to solve her problems, nor help to keep from making the same old mistakes all over again. It did not tell her when to stay and fight, and when to accept that something simply wasn't going to work out, no matter how much she wanted it.

It didn't tell her what to do now, she thought as she turned toward the window, and lay looking out at the darkness of the night. Because now it wasn't just she and Trace who stood to be really hurt and disappointed if things didn't work out, their four boys were involved, too. They were swiftly becoming a unified group. As much as they all longed for a complete family again, it would be hell, giving them that, then having to take it away....

"I can't believe it's still raining this hard," he murmured after a while.

Neither could Susannah. It was a tempest. "Do you think we should call the boys?"

"It wouldn't hurt to check on them." Trace picked up the hunting-lodge telephone on the nightstand and punched in a number. He sat up against the headboard, the sheet pulled up to his waist. "Hi, Nate. How are things at the house?" He paused, listening intently, then said affably, "Sure. Put her on."

Her? Susannah thought.

"Hi." Trace listened some more. A worried frown began to crease his handsome face.

Susannah was not used to being cut out of the action. "What's going on?" she whispered anxiously.

"Hold on a minute, Gillian." Trace rested the phone on his shoulder and covered the receiver with his palm. "Gillian Taylor stopped by the lake house a while ago, hoping to wait out the worst of the storm—she said she was out driving and got caught in it. She said we've got high water in several places on the ranch, and there are several places where the Silver River is spilling out of its banks."

In the background, Susannah and Trace could hear the boys conferring excitedly with the new logging-camp chef. Their questions all came at once: "Is it white water now?" "What happens if it keeps flooding?" "Can we see the river?" "Does it look cool or just scary?"

Trace put the receiver back to his ear. "Gillian, tell the boys that I'll take them to see the river tomorrow, when the danger passes. Until then, they are not to go near it," he ordered firmly.

He waited while Gillian relayed the message.

As Trace continued to listen, he began to relax. "All right," he said eventually. "Yes, I agree, that's probably best. We'll see you in the morning."

The morning?

"Okay, 'bye."

"What do you mean we'll see them in the morning?" Susannah repeated, shocked, as soon as Trace hung up.

"Gillian offered to stay with the boys until we could get back tomorrow morning. Since driving conditions are treacherous at best at the moment, I said okay."

"Without conferring with me first?" Susannah asked, beginning to feel a little irritated.

"We have no choice."

Susannah sighed. She had thought things were different. That this time they would be equal partners. Now she wasn't so sure. Though she had no doubt he cared for her in his way, Trace seemed to be simply taking over everything. Telling all four boys what they could and could not do. Deciding the two of them would stay the night in the hunting lodge without even asking her what she wanted to do. In buying her the computer and putting the new software on it, he had even inserted himself in her business life.

Of course, the new computer and software would make her upcoming consulting job a lot easier, not to mention the writing of her cookbook series. And she did appreciate the help with the boys, Susannah conceded reluctantly to herself. But that wasn't the point. The point was, he was completely taking over her life again, as effortlessly as he'd done before, and it had only taken him thirty-two hours. What would it be like in thirty-two days, or thirty-two weeks? Would she end up feeling as incidental to their life together as she had before? And how would she cope with that if it did happen? she wondered bleakly.

As the storm continued to rage outside, Trace studied her expression. Finally, he said patiently, "If you have another option, I'm willing to listen."

That was just it, Susannah thought with a beleaguered sigh as she climbed from the bed. They didn't have any other options. Of course, she had put herself in this position, Susannah thought as she pulled on a satin robe she found in the closet. She knew to give Trace an inch was to give him a mile. Turning away, she did her best to hide the tumult swirling inside her, the fear that nothing had really changed between them, after all. "No, I don't."

"Well, then..." Trace frowned abruptly as he pulled on a pair of loose-fitting pajama pants he found in one of the bureau drawers. "Damn," he muttered, a distracted faraway look in his blue eyes.

Susannah started. Something was up. Something that obviously didn't include her. "What?" she prodded.

"I need to tell my attorney the Farraday deal is on again. I better call him."

Business again, even as midnight approached.

Tamping down her disappointment, she watched as Trace picked up the telephone again. "We're going to need a notary to witness the transaction, too," he murmured.

Trace started to dial, then studied the expression on her face, and stopped mid-dial before he said, "The more I do to set things up this evening, the smoother things will run tomorrow morning."

Susannah knew that. She even understood it. She told herself she was being childish. She could handle Trace's devotion to business this time around, provided he made time for her and the boys, too. She slipped her hands inside the pockets of her robe. "I wanted to take a hot bath, anyway."

He nodded, his mind on business again. "I'll be in to keep you company as soon as I finish."

Wondering if he would keep that promise, or disappoint her yet again, Susannah slipped into the adjacent bathroom, filled the claw-foot tub with bubbles and hot water, and lit some candles. She had wanted to honor Max's wishes without getting emotionally involved with Trace again. But she'd gotten involved anyway. She had wanted to think that the second-honeymoon phase of their relationship would last a little longer. But that wasn't happening, either, Susannah thought with a troubled sigh. The simple truth was that she and Trace had been romantically reunited for little more than a day and it was already back to business as usual. With Trace absorbed in his work and her left yearning for more.

Of course, this time around it would be different since she had her own work and the four children to sustain her, but still, Susannah thought as she sank even deeper into the frothy bubbles, she would've thought Trace would do a little better, at least until after she had a wedding ring on her finger again. But maybe this was exactly the kind of reality check she needed before the ceremony. Maybe this was what she needed to keep her from wallowing in self-pity and disappointment once more. Heaven knew, she didn't want to set her expectations too high again, only to feel hurt and disillusioned.

No sooner had she made up her mind to proceed a little more cautiously where she and Trace were concerned, than there was a simultaneous flash of lightning and a deafening crack of thunder, and then the lights went out.

"Oh, no," Susannah moaned, knowing from experience that when the electricity went out in the country, as it was wont to do during any kind of storm, it could be hours before it came on again.

"Susannah? You okay?" Trace shouted from the living room.

"Fine," she shouted back.

Moments later, he appeared in the doorway, charging in like a white knight to the rescue, flashlight in hand. As the beam swept over her, highlighting the silky glow of her skin and the curves of her breasts, she flushed self-consciously, and sank a little lower in the bubbles.

"I wonder if the lights went out at the lake house, too," she murmured.

"Probably." Trace let his glance trail over her lazily. "Our telephone line is out, as well—it cut me off midconversation—and we can't use the cell phone during the storm, but I'll see if I can get the boys on the shortwave radio."

Moments later, he returned, looking supremely happy and relaxed. "I got through. Gillian says everything is fine, though their lights and telephone are also out." He grinned. "*They* think it's a hell of an adventure."

Susannah could imagine. "Thank heavens Gillian is there with them," she murmured, unspeakably relieved.

"Even if she weren't, I think they would do okay," Trace said confidently as his glance roved her with male appreciation. "But you're right, it is a relief, knowing we have an adult there to watch over them."

Trace strode back out. She presumed to finish his business via shortwave radio this time.

Seconds later, he returned, carrying a silver bucket and tray. Susannah gaped as he shucked his pajama pants, poured them both a second glass of champagne and climbed in opposite her. There was something to be said for the lights going out, the phone lines being down and business being made impossible, after all, she thought.

"You look surprised," Trace noted as he settled opposite her.

Susannah sipped her champagne and relaxed against the curved back of the tub. "I am."

She'd swept her hair up off the back of her neck. Tendrils escaped to frame the heat-flushed contours of her oval face. The candlelight cast a luminous glow over her damp, silky skin. Excitement glimmered in her dark eyes. She knew they were going to make love again, Trace thought with satisfaction, and she wanted the intimacy as much as he did. Just as she—like he—wanted this relationship of theirs to work.

He smiled and drank deeply of his own champagne. "I decided the power and phone going off when they did was a sign, probably from Uncle Max. Business can wait, Susannah." Trace set aside his glass and hers and leaned forward to take her in his arms and give her a champagne-flavored kiss. "This can't."

Trace picked up a bath sponge and drew the soap across it, once, twice. He transferred the soap to her skin. She sucked in her breath as the bubbles floated across her shoulders, down her back, over her rib cage to her breasts.

''Nor can this.'' She picked up the soap, lathered her palms and spread them across his chest, her nimble fingers ghosting over his skin until fire flowed through him in undulating waves.

Trace smiled as he abandoned the sponge in lieu of his hands. ''Sometimes the simplest way is best.'' He found the insides of her thighs beneath the water and spread soap across them, too.

Susannah sucked in her breath. ''Trace.''

''Feel good?''

She lathered her hands again and with soft, gliding motions, transferred the soap to the insides of his thighs. ''Does this?''

Trace groaned and shuddered in response as she sudsed the rest of him, too. 'You know it does.'' Scooting her closer so she was astride him, he soaped his way down her back, past the nip of her waist, to the curves of her hips. Holding her securely across his thighs, he kissed her deeply, thoroughly, transferring all their earlier uncertainty into the kind of desire that took hours and hours of steady, sensual lovemaking to satisfy. His hands skimmed upward to cup her breasts as she wrapped her arms around his neck. ''I could stay like this all evening,'' he murmured contentedly.

So could she, Susannah thought. Her smile curved against his. ''The water might get cold,'' she warned as a deep warmth spread through her.

''Not with the kind of heat we're generating, it won't.'' He wrapped her legs around his waist. Then he cupped her buttocks and kissed her with gathering urgency. She had meant to hold off, to make it last and last, but the minute his fingers found her, she took off into a thousand shimmering sensations. And as the feelings swept her, as he lifted her and moved deep inside her once again, she knew no one would ever make her feel the way he did.

Trace surged inside her knowing if they made love all night long it would never be enough. The desire he felt for Susannah was unlike anything he had ever known, as was the soft, sensual feel of her mouth melding to his. Her body still pulsing with reaction, she wrapped her arms around him, silently offering him anything he wanted, needed. And what he needed, Trace thought as she cradled his head between her palms, kissing his face and then his throat, was her. Only her. And then he was over the edge, too. Exploding in a searing flash that hurtled them both into the sweetness of oblivion, into the sweetness of being together once again.

And when the tremors stopped, Trace gently kissed Susannah, dried her off, carried her to the bed and started all over again.

TRACE HELD Susannah close, long after the tremors from their last bout of lovemaking had subsided. She slept, her head against his chest, her body curled against his. It had been years since he had felt so content, yet he was worried, too. He knew Susannah loved him, just as he loved her, even though they had yet to say the words, but he had only to look into her eyes to see how wary she still was. He knew he had failed her once in not being there the way she needed him, when she needed him. He didn't want to do so again.

Chapter Ten

9:07

Susannah woke to the sound of Trace's voice. She couldn't make out most of the words, but she knew from the disgruntled sound of his low voice that whatever he was dealing with was not good news. Alarmed, she sat up against the headboard. The rain had stopped an hour or so before. The first light of dawn was filtering in beneath the bedroom drapes. "What's going on?" she asked as soon as he had turned off his cell phone and come back into the bedroom to join her.

Clad only in his silk boxers, Trace sat down beside her. Though it was only a little past six in the morning, and the two of them had been up most of the night making love over and over again, he had already showered and shaved. His hair was slicked back. The scent of soap clung to his skin. He looked sexy, and to her disappointment, preoccupied.

"I finished the calls I was unable to make last night. There's no way everyone can get out to the ranch this morning to sign the papers on the Farraday deal, so we've changed the site to the Fort Benton Gentlemen's

Club. Not to worry. The meeting is still on for 9:00 a.m. That'll give us plenty of time to make it back here for the ceremony.''

Susannah blinked, wondering where she fit into this, even as she cleared her mind of sleep. ''Us?''

''It'll take more than thirty minutes just to get to town and back,'' Trace explained, pouring her a cup of coffee from the carafe on a tray. Their hands touched as he stirred a lavish amount of cream into the aromatic brew and fit the mug into her cupped hands. ''Because of Max's will, you'll have to go with me.''

It was their wedding day. And Trace was concerned mainly about business. Susannah pushed aside her disappointment and struggled not to feel resentful as she sipped the delicious coffee. This deal was important to Trace, she reminded herself sternly, and he had told her last night he intended to sign those sale papers today. ''I want to take the boys with us,'' she cautioned, taking another long enervating sip. She felt they had neglected the children enough the past twenty-four hours.

Trace quaffed his own coffee. ''No problem,'' he told her as she headed for the shower. ''We'll stop by to get them at the same time we pick up some business clothes.''

Half an hour later, they passed a telephone truck working to restore phone service to the area, and pulled into the lake house driveway. By the time they reached the rambling house, Gillian, alerted they were en route via Trace's cell phone, was waiting for them on the front porch. As Susannah and Trace stepped from his Jeep, she smiled and reported, ''The boys have already had cold cereal, fruit and milk—it's all I could do to get them to sit still long enough to eat. I've got to get over to the logging-camp dining hall to supervise the breakfast shift."

"Thanks for staying last night."

"No problem." Gillian looked relaxed and at ease. "It was fun."

"Where are the boys now?" Susannah glanced around, surprised by the silence. There was no stereo blasting from the upstairs windows—though she might have Gillian to thank for that.

Gillian inclined her head in the direction of the backyard. "They're looking over the tree branches knocked down by the storm last night. Listen, gotta run."

"Thanks again, Gillian," Trace said.

As soon as Gillian took off, Trace and Susannah hurried around to the back. To their mutual dismay, the boys' clothes were covered with a mixture of rain-water, mud and grass stains. To take them anywhere would require them all to shower first.

"Can we go see the white water?" Scott asked. "We heard on the shortwave this morning that the water is rising fast upstream from here."

"Maybe later," Susannah said.

"If we have time," Trace added.

The boys' faces reflected their collective disappointment.

"We have to go into town," Susannah continued. "Trace has to sign some business papers."

Nate grinned as he pushed his glasses farther up on the bridge of his nose. "Hey, Dad. The Farraday deal come through for you, after all?"

"Sure did," Trace reported, looking equally pleased.

"Cool," Jason said, giving Trace a high five.

"Yeah, cool," Mickey parroted, also giving Trace a high five, though it was clear the eight-year-old had no idea what they were talking about.

"We were going to ask you guys to go with us," Trace said. The high fives completed, he glanced at his watch. "But we're on a tight schedule."

Nate and Scott exchanged glances that were almost brotherly they were so telepathic.

"How long are you going to be gone?" Scott asked casually.

"Three, maybe four hours. We should be home by noon at the latest."

The boys exchanged noncommittal looks. No one seemed upset about their parents' slated absence. "No problem," Scott said easily.

"We'll stay here and clean up the branches in the yard," Nate volunteered.

"And we'll help," Jason added, while Mickey nodded.

Again, Susannah had the sense that things were going almost too well. But Trace, his mind clearly on the business ahead of them, apparently picked up no such vibes. He glanced at his watch again. "They are still working on the phone lines, though I expect service will be restored soon. Meantime, you boys have your cell phone with you in case I need to reach you or vice versa?" Nate nodded and pulled the slim, folded telephone from his shirt pocket with the button flap. "Good," Trace said with an approving smile. "Susannah and I will run up and change clothes. Then we'll be on our way. Would you like us to bring you some lunch from town? Pizza or—"

"Pizza," the boys said in unison.

"Okay then." A hand already to her spine, Trace gently propelled Susannah in the direction of the house. "We'll be back by noon," he promised the boys.

8:20

SUSANNAH AND TRACE did not talk much on the way into town. He was on his cell phone with his attorney, going over the contract for the sale. And they were still talking when Trace parked in front of the Fort Benton Gentlemen's Club, an elegantly preserved building in the historic district. Trace finished his conversation, and hung up the phone. "I'll try to wrap this up as quickly as I can," he promised.

Susannah nodded. The night before had been wonderfully romantic and satisfying. This morning was like a replay of their old harried life together, each of them moving in different spheres. At least they would be, Susannah thought, as soon as the clause in Max's will, forcing them to stick to each other like glue, expired.

"Keeping in mind Max's stipulation we remain under one roof, I've arranged for you to have one of the private reading rooms on the second floor, while the meeting goes on in an adjacent conference room. But if you'd prefer to use our last thirty-minute time-out and go shopping in one of the stores here instead," Trace suggested, aiming to please.

"No. The reading room will be fine," Susannah said. Maybe there she could calm the jitters inside her.

Swift minutes later, she found herself cozily ensconced in the room just down the hall from Trace,

Sam Farraday and their two attorneys. Trace had thoughtfully arranged for a stack of magazines and a continental breakfast to be sent to Susannah, but as she read the latest editions of *Redbook, Newsweek* and *Bon Appetite,* and then started on a second stack of magazines, her mind kept wandering to the boys. She was glad they were all getting along so well, but she missed them, and felt she and Trace hadn't spent nearly enough time with them the past couple of days, under the circumstances. Deciding there was no time like the present to make up for that, and find out what the kids wanted on the pizza from town they had requested for lunch, which would need to be ordered soon if they were going to have it home by noon, as promised, she picked up the phone and dialed the lake house. She was relieved to find the house phone lines were up and running again. She let it ring a dozen times, hung up and dialed again. Still no answer. Remembering the boys had a cell phone with them outside, Susannah slipped back to the meeting room. She knocked, and when admitted, apologized for the interruption. Everyone frowned. Ignoring their dismay, she asked, "Trace, what is the number for the boys?"

He rattled off the lake house number. She shook her head. She already had that. "Their cell-phone number." Trace rattled that off, too. She wrote it down, on a FBGC notepad, thanked him and retired to her private reading room, where she tried again. And again got no answer. Not the first time, nor the second, nor the third.

Frowning, Susannah tried the lake house. The cell phone. The lake house. The cell phone. She thought about the vicious storm the evening before, the water rising upstream, and tried not to panic, and failed mightily. Something was wrong, she just knew it.

7:01

AT THE SOUND of the knocking, Trace glanced up irritably again. Looking at the disgruntled faces around him—he couldn't blame them for resenting the interruption—he stood. "I'll get it."

He opened the door. Seeing Susannah there, looking incredibly beautiful in a white linen business suit and pearls, did little to ease the mounting frustration emanating from the room. Shutting the door behind him, he stepped out into the hall. "What now, Susannah?" he demanded impatiently.

Her sable brown eyes narrowed at his tone, but she plunged on, anyway, announcing flatly, "Something's wrong. I can't get hold of the boys."

"Did you try the lake house?"

Susannah nodded, but she kept her eyes on his as she related anxiously, "And the cell phone. Repeatedly. They're not answering."

Trace frowned. At ten and fourteen, Nate and Jason were old enough and mature enough to be left alone. There had never been a problem thus far. He had no reason to think there was a problem this morning. "They're probably playing that Hootie and The Blowfish CD at top volume again and can't hear the rings of either."

Susannah paused, and bit her lip. Apparently, Trace thought, she hadn't thought of that. "Now, if you don't mind, I want to go back to—"

She flattened a hand across the portal, blocking his way back inside the conference room. She tilted her chin at him defiantly. "I want to go back to the ranch, Trace."

"Fine. Just give me another fifteen minutes to wrap this up."

"Take your fifteen minutes. Just give me the keys to your Jeep. As you reminded me earlier, we have one time-out left. I want to use it. Now."

Aware his own emotions were skyrocketing, he blew out an exasperated sigh. "Susannah—"

"Fine." She spun on her heel. Hands curled into fists at her sides, she marched away from him. "If you don't want to help me, I'll call a cab."

Trace caught up with her in two short strides and blocked her way. His frown deepening, he reached into his pocket and pressed the keys into her hand. "Take the Jeep, Susannah. But wait for me." If there was trouble, as she suspected, he wanted to be there, too. "I'll be down in five minutes, max."

SUSANNAH HEADED for the Jeep, taking their last and final time-out from each other. Pulse racing with a mixture of apprehension over the boys and anger at Trace for his insistence on putting his business deal ahead of the welfare of their children, she climbed behind the wheel, inserted the key in the ignition and picked up the cell phone once again. Dialed repeatedly, hoping she would be proven wrong, Trace right. But once again, there was no answer either place. And there was no sign of Trace. Four minutes had already passed. Then five. Six.

To hell with it. She was not just going to sit here, waiting until all the "i's" were dotted, the "t's" crossed, when their boys' very lives could be at stake.

She started the Jeep, and pulled out into the light traffic peppering Main Street, praying all the while that everything really would turn out to be all right.

Some fifteen minutes later, halfway to the ranch, Susannah became aware of a pickup truck behind her. It was gaining fast. As the distance between them on the long, lonely highway closed, she saw why. His attorney was behind the wheel, Trace beside him. The attorney honked. Trace motioned for her to pull over. She had half a mind to ignore them both. Only her reluctance to put Trace's attorney in the middle of her disagreement with Trace, as her quarreling parents had often done to her, made her reconsider.

Scowling all the while, she reluctantly pulled over.

Trace got out, and circled to the front of the truck. Not on the passenger side. But the driver's side. "Thanks for waiting," he told her sarcastically.

"I waited five minutes. And then some," Susannah said as she slid across the console to the passenger side.

Trace got in behind the wheel. Checking behind him and finding it clear, he thrust the Jeep into gear and swung out onto the highway again. "Have you tried to reach the boys again?"

"Yes." She fastened her seat belt, then folded her arms in front of her. "With absolutely no luck. You?"

"The same."

Susannah released an unsteady breath as her eyes scanned the horizon. "If they are in trouble, I am never going to forgive myself," she muttered.

He slanted her a clear, direct look. "If they are in trouble, and it is—as I suspect—the kind of trouble that could be easily avoided because they know better, then you aren't the one who is going to need to be forgiven, Susannah. They are."

Susannah had no answer to that, so she fell silent. And concentrated instead on any signs of Medivac choppers whirling about.

Excruciatingly long moments later, Trace turned into the driveway of the lake house. The yard was oddly silent. No stereo was playing. The debris from the storm had been cleared up and was neatly stacked at one corner of the yard, but the boys were nowhere in sight.

They split up, exploring the inside and outside of the house, and met again in the kitchen. "Anyone in here?"

"No." Susannah paused, fighting panic. "Any sign of them in the yard?"

"No," Trace reported grimly. "Nor were they at the dock, or in the woods adjacent to us."

Nothing bad had happened to their boys. They were just misbehaving—again. "They have to be around here somewhere," Susannah persisted.

Trace seemed to agree. "Did you check the garage?"

"There was no one there, either."

"What about their fishing gear?"

"I didn't think to look to see if it was there or not." Susannah laid a hand across her chest as the next thought occurred to her. "Oh, God, Trace." She lifted her eyes to his, anguish sweeping through her in debilitating waves. "You don't think they went down to the stream again."

"After the kind of storm we had last night, and the flooding that's already happened in various places around the ranch, they definitely know better—but it would also explain why they were so happy to see us go off again this morning."

"And they were pressing us to let them go see the white water," Susannah recalled.

Trace opened the door to the storeroom behind the garage where the gear had been stored, and scowled. "Just as I thought. The fishing poles and inner tubes are gone."

Susannah felt faint. "I didn't even know they had inner tubes!"

"They weren't inflated. Nate and Jason occasionally use them when they swim."

Susannah had a vision of churning white water. All the blood left her face. "Oh, God, Trace. You don't think they—"

"Went to see how high the river got overnight? That's exactly what I think, Susannah. Worse—" Trace picked up the cell phone from the garage floor "—they forgot to take this with them."

"Which means not only are they in a potentially dangerous situation, they're incommunicado," she murmured, terrified.

"Exactly." Swearing his frustration, Trace grabbed a rope and a couple of blankets from the garage and set off through the woods in the direction of the fishing hole. She grabbed the cell phone and ran to catch up with him. As they moved through the woods, she reminded herself how bright the boys were. "I'm sure they're all right," she told Trace, doing her best to stay calm. Nothing would be gained if she became hysterical.

"You haven't seen that river after a hard rain. It's nothing but swirling white water."

Which was, no doubt, exactly what their boys had gone to see. Susannah swallowed hard. She could feel the anger building inside her head. "You don't think they would try to innertube down it, do you?"

"I hope not. My boys know better." He slanted her a glance. "Do yours? Damn it, Susannah, if I had raised *my* son, he damn well would have known better!"

She flinched. "What's that supposed to mean?" She knew they shouldn't be fighting; she couldn't help it.

Trace's lips compressed into a thin white line. "It means, if you had taught Scott and Mickey to follow orders from the outset, or instilled any discipline in them whatsoever we would not be in this situation."

"Like hell we wouldn't." Her voice rose to match his. "You're the one who couldn't stop talking about the joys of living out in the wilderness, Trace. The one who had them all fishing in the river yesterday, the one who wouldn't take them to see the white water this morning when they asked and why?—because you had to cinch a business deal!"

Trace's mouth set grimly. He did not deny he had missed the signs of impending mischief cum disaster. "Nevertheless," he said, his tone roughening accusingly, "Nate and Jason would never disobey my orders and sneak away on their own."

Susannah snorted as she struggled to keep pace. "I doubt Scott and Mickey had to twist Nate and Jason's arms. Face it, they all wanted to see the river, and they knew with us being away all morning tending to your latest business acquisition, and the wedding this afternoon, that we wouldn't have time to go today.'' Not that this was the only problem they were facing. Clearly, Trace still resented her not telling him about his son. She'd thought—hoped—they could get over this and move on, the way Max had wanted. Now she wasn't so sure. Damn Trace for waiting until this moment to confront her.

They tore through the trees and stopped just short of the fishing hole. Water was spilling out of the banks in a swirling torrent.

"Oh, God," Susannah gasped, staring at the churning foaming whitecaps on the gray-brown water. She couldn't hide an involuntary shudder. "You don't think they took inner tubes and actually went into that."

Ignoring the possibility altogether, Trace indicated the muddy shoe-prints leading upriver. "Let's hope these lead us to the boys."

As they rounded the bend in the river, Susannah saw smoke billowing above the trees. How a fire was possible, when the woods were drenched, she didn't know. Her heart jolted. Tensing from head to toe, she grabbed Trace's arm and pointed in the direction of her gaze. "What's that?" she demanded.

Trace peered at it. "I'll be damned," he muttered, looking both surprised and alarmed.

"What?"

"Nate is sending us smoke signals." Trace quickened his pace.

"And?"

"They're in trouble," he said, breaking into a run. "Big trouble."

"DAD! Dad! Over here!" Nate shouted as Trace and Susannah swept into view.

Susannah gasped. The boys were crowded together in the middle of what had once been a long wide sandbar in the middle of the river. They had their fishing gear with them. On either side of them was churning white water that seemed to be steadily rising. All four of them were bare-chested. Two of their shirts and the wooden tackle box were the basis for the fire they'd made. The other two shirts were being used to create the short bursts of smoke that had led to their rescue.

"Get your belts off," Trace yelled, already tying one end of the rope to a tree. He tied the other end around his waist. Terrified, Susannah watched as Trace waded in the four feet of swirling water. She could see that the powerful force of the water was threatening to knock him off his feet, even though it was only waist-high on him. He reached the sandbar. Grabbing Mickey, who was the youngest and smallest, he snapped, "All of you, get your belts around your waists, like this, and then fasten them around the rope like a safety line. That's it. That's good. Then we're all going to wade back to the other side. I want you holding tight to the rope and each other," he instructed fiercely.

"It's gonna sweep us away," Mickey cried.

"No, it's not," Trace said sternly, still holding tight to Mickey. "Scott, you take the lead. Nate, you got next. Then Jason. Then Mickey and me."

It took two minutes for them all to get across. It was the longest two minutes of Susannah's life as she watched them struggle across in tandem, being nearly knocked off their feet, catching each other, persevering. And all the while, the water kept swirling and rising.

Finally, Scott reached the bank. Susannah grabbed hold of the rope still attached to the tree and him and helped pull him to safety. She and Scott helped pull Jason to safety, and so on, until everyone was out of the water, and on the bank. Trace rapidly untied the rope from the tree. "Let's go. Now. This river could break loose at any minute," he said.

Exhausted, trembling, they headed off through the woods. Seconds later, there was a roar. And then the sandbank, too, was completely covered with swirling, churning white water.

"BEFORE YOU YELL AT US," an exhausted-looking Scott said as the four of them reached the house and plopped down on the lawn, "you need to understand it was all my fault. I thought it would be fun to toss in a fishing line when the river was so wild."

"If you blame him, you have to blame all of us," Nate interjected. " 'Cause we all wanted to go."

"Yeah, we were planning it all night, whenever Gillian wasn't around," Jason said.

"As soon as you guys left this morning," Mickey said through chattering teeth, "we hurried up and finished cleaning up the branches in the yard and then we left."

"So, we're to understand it was one for all, all for one?" Trace said sternly.

The four boys nodded.

"Then your punishment will be one for all, all for one, too," Trace declared, without even looking at Susannah, who was still shaking with thoughts of what might have happened if she and Trace hadn't come along when they did. What if they had waited for Trace's business to be completed? What if she hadn't given in to instinct and telephoned, and kept on telephoning? What then? Would their boys have been swept into the wildly churning river, and . . . ? She felt the blood drain out of her face, inch by inch, until she knew she was bone-white.

"But we'll talk about what your punishment is going to be later," Trace said. "Right now, I want everyone upstairs and into the showers—now. Put on some warm clothes and then come right back down," Trace instructed.

"Yes, sir!" Clearly shaken by the morning's events, the boys scrambled to obey.

Susannah stared at Trace. It wasn't just the shock. Never had she felt more unnecessary and extraneous in her life.

3:20

AWARE HE WAS DRIPPING river water everywhere, Trace headed for his bedroom, too. To his surprise, Susannah followed him. Her expression was stormy. "We need to get something cleared up before you say anything else to the boys," she told him bluntly.

Trace stripped off his wet clothes. He knew she was upset. He didn't blame her. He was upset, as well. Their children's impetuous behavior could have easily cost them their lives. "No problem. Just give me a minute—" He turned on the shower and stepped in.

"Now, Trace." Susannah stepped into the bathroom after him. "Where do you get off treating me that way?" she demanded imperiously.

As the warm water washed over his shoulders, Trace regarded her with astonishment. "What way?"

Susannah leaned back against the bathroom wall and folded her arms in front of her. "Why did you wait until now—until after we'd made love again and again—to let me know how you really feel?" she said in a soft, disparaging voice.

Trace shook his head. "What are you talking about?"

"Your accusation that this wouldn't have happened if you had raised Scott." Chin up, she slanted him a reproachful look.

"I'm sorry I said that. I was upset. What matters is, the boys are safe," he said calmly as he soaped his chest, then his shoulders.

"No one is more glad of that than I am."

"But...?" Trace prompted, sensing there was more as he turned slightly toward the shower, letting the water sluice over him in a steady, cleansing stream.

Susannah released a frustrated breath. "What about us? How can you say what you did and then act like everything is still okay?" she asked, hurt.

Trace shrugged as he began to soap the lower half of his body. "Because it is."

She kept her eyes averted, even as she paled at the remark. "Is it, Trace?" Susannah said very quietly, the hint of angry tears adding a luminous quality to her sable brown eyes.

She started to step away, but with a hand on her shoulder he pulled her back. In the past, he would've let her go. Now, there was no way. "What are you trying to tell me?" he demanded quietly.

She shoved at his chest with both hands, pushing him away. "That nothing has changed!" Susannah stormed, her voice rising emotionally. "We're still all wrong for each other."

Giving him no chance to disagree, she plunged on, "I put family first. You put your business first. And when it comes to our personal life, you still want to call all the shots, make all the decisions. Marriage for you isn't a partnership, Trace, at least not the way it should be, it's a solo act." Eyes flashing, her jaw set, she continued accusingly, "And you picked a hell of a time to vent your fury at me for not telling you about Scott."

Trace put the soap aside. "I already told you, I lost my temper."

"You spoke the truth."

Trace watched the way her lower lip quivered with hurt and fought the urge to simply take her in his arms and kiss her and make love to her until the hurt went away. "So what are you saying, Susannah?" he asked, wanting to get this matter settled as much as she did.

"That I have to forget what you told me about Scott in order to be with you."

She paled. "Of course not!"

"Then what?" Trace shut off the water and grabbed a towel. He wrapped it around his waist.

She sagged against the wall, watching him, keeping her eyes level on his. "I want to feel like we've put the past behind us."

"We have," Trace insisted.

She cleared her throat as she straightened. The damp heat of the shower had her clothes clinging to her as she calmly, coolly disagreed, "No, we haven't. And, in fact, you don't know that in here—" Susannah splayed her palms across his bare chest, and pointed to his heart, "—and that scares me."

"It shouldn't," Trace said gently.

Before she knew what was happening, he had one hand threaded through her hair, the other on her spine. He was kissing her with a thoroughness and a passion that took her breath away. And she was kissing him back, until she suddenly realized that he was doing it again, using the physical passion they felt for each other to get his way whenever they disagreed.

Furious, she tore her mouth from his and pulled away. "I can't do this, Trace." Tears stung her eyes and clogged her throat. "I can't pretend everything is okay when it's not." She dragged a hand through her hair, pushing the damp, mussed strands off her face. Her throat aching, she shook her head and pushed past him. Opened the door and stepped out of the shower stall.

Trace followed her into the bedroom. He watched as she perched wearily on the edge of the bed.

"Look, maybe everything has happened too soon," he said after a moment. "Maybe we should just acquiesce to Max's wishes and go to the South Pacific, have that honeymoon we denied ourselves years ago and take it one day at a time." He wanted this to work with all his heart and soul. He had thought Susannah did, too. It hurt to discover that didn't appear to be the case, that she was ready to run away again at the first sign of difficulty.

She turned tormented eyes to his. "Do you really think we're ready for that?" she asked sadly.

"I think we were ready years ago," Trace told her firmly as he closed the distance between them. "We just didn't know it. And because we didn't know it, we didn't try nearly hard enough to hold on to what we had."

Susannah ducked her head and didn't disagree with that. "What if it doesn't work out this time?"

With just a matter of hours left until the wedding, Trace knew he had to lay the groundwork for their future before any more time passed. A large part of that was his fault, and his alone. He knew he hadn't been fair with Susannah in the past, nor had he been fair with her at the beginning of their forty-eight hours together again.

It was important, he felt, that she realize he was determined to do better in the future. It was important that he reassure her. He knelt in front of her and took her hand in his. "Look, I know I forced you into this arrangement of ours, at least initially. I know today has been a mess from start to finish so far, and that everything is happening awfully fast. But I think our relationship can work, with or without a written marriage contract."

A chill went through Susannah. Once again, Trace sounded as if he was negotiating a business deal. One that involved his family instead of timberland. She pushed away from the bed and began to pace. "It's not just us who stand to be hurt if it doesn't work out this time, Trace. If we attempt to have a real marriage, and fail, the boys will be hurt, too." She shook her head, the regret she felt almost overwhelming her. "They already feel like brothers...to give that to them, in a real meaningful sense, then take it away after all they've already been through...losing one parent to illness..." She didn't see how they could do it.

Trace watched her move to the window and look out at the still, quiet mountain lake. "They won't get hurt if we don't let them get hurt."

Susannah feared they couldn't protect them. She began to pace again, her arms folded in front of her. "Once again, you're not listening to me, Trace. I don't want them in the middle of our problems," she told him tautly.

His expression gentle, he came up behind her and massaged the tension from her shoulders. "They don't have to be. If we have anything to say, anything that needs hashing out, we'll do it with each other, and we'll do it when we're alone, plain and simple."

He made it sound so easy. Susannah knew it wasn't. The boys had already picked up on the romance between them, they would pick up on the troubles, too. And if their romance could please and elate them, their troubles would depress and devastate them. Struggling not to give in to the gentle ministrations of his hands, she swung around to face him. "If you find you can't forget what I've done...

Trace spread his hands and shrugged. "Then we'll give ourselves the necessary space from each other, until we can get along again."

Which meant what? she wondered, feeling even more lost and hurt. That he would hide in his office while she seethed in hers? It sounded as if he'd written himself an out-clause, just in case.

"We have all the components to make this relationship of ours work, Susannah," Trace continued gently. "Because of Max's generosity, you're going to be able to write your cookbooks and I'll have the biggest logging outfit in the West. Between us, our four boys will have a mom and a dad, and we've got the lake house to bring them up in. I know there will be problems getting adjusted to each other again, but in the end it'll be great, you'll see. And we'll know we've done what we should have done for Scott, a long time ago."

He was talking about duty. But what about love? Susannah wondered, feeling all the more upset by Trace's careful recitation. Wasn't a deep and abiding love part of the equation for a successful marriage, too? Or was this Trace's subtle way of telling her that there was to be no love in their relationship this time around? Only passion and a burning desire to make things work, if only so he could be with the son he had never known he had.

TRACE WASN'T SURE how or why. He just knew he had failed again. Susannah had awakened happy and ready to face the day. Now she was tense and unhappy again, in the same way she had been during their marriage. Once again, he had failed her, without even knowing how or why, when all he had been trying to do was apologize for what he had said and make things better between them. They were silent as they continued to face off. Finally, he said, "I've disappointed you, haven't I?"

His question brought another weary sigh. Desperate to save the situation, Trace took her unresisting body into his arms and plunged on, "Look, I know romantic relationships are not my forte," he told her as he ran his palms up and down her chilled arms, seeking to generate some warmth. "We've been over that. But I know from experience that I can make a marriage work on a practical level now, even without a burning romance."

His statement had her eyebrows lifting. Realizing too late it had been a mistake alluding to his second wife, Trace cursed himself. Trailing his hands down her arms, to her wrists, he took her hands in his, looked deep into Susannah's eyes and continued painstakingly, methodically building his case. "Our life together may not be all passion, fun and excitement." In his view, no marriage was that. "But it can be steady and satisfying. And that should not be discounted."

But obviously it wasn't enough for her, Trace thought, studying her increasingly unhappy expression as she coolly withdrew her hands from his and stepped back and away from him.

He had never seen her so tense, he thought, as she gave him a taut, troubled smile that did not begin to reach her eyes.

"Nor can we discount the fact that if we try this and fail, we will end up being every bit as miserable and unhappy as we were when we were married the first time. Only this time, the boys will be miserable right along with us," Susannah concluded sadly.

There was no arguing that; Trace knew to fail again would devastate everyone.

"What are you saying?" Trace asked, afraid deep in his gut he already knew, as the tightness in her eyes and around her mouth became more pronounced.

Susannah gazed morosely up at him and drew a deep breath. "That I'll go through with the wedding ceremony so you can inherit, and allow you unlimited access to Scott because I think I owe you that at the very least. But as for the rest of it, Trace, the marriage is off, it has to be."

Chapter Eleven

1:59

"It's our fault Mom has locked herself in her bedroom, isn't it?" the boys asked as Trace flipped turkey burgers from the griddle onto a serving platter. "She's mad 'cause we got stuck in the middle of the river and almost got killed."

"No, guys, she's mad at me."

"Why? What'd you do besides rescue us?"

Trace's behavior hadn't been exemplary all along, he reluctantly admitted to himself as he watched the boys liberally apply ketchup, mustard and pickles to their burgers. He had, after all, blackmailed her into the idea of staying married to him, for Scott's sake. Knowing how independent Susannah had become in their years apart, she couldn't have taken too kindly to that.

"It's complicated," Trace said finally as he set out pitchers of milk and apple juice.

"Which really means you don't know, right?" Mickey said.

"In that case, don't you think you should find out?" Scott suggested helpfully.

"I agree," Nate added gravely between gulps of juice. "As long as you're in the doghouse, Dad, you might as well know why."

"And right away," Jason added seriously.

1:30

TAKING A CUE from the boys, Trace knocked on the bedroom door. It would have been amusing to find himself taking relationship advice from children, if there hadn't been quite so much at stake. "Susannah, the guys and I prepared lunch for you."

She opened the door, her expression cautious. "Where are the boys?"

"Downstairs, eating." Which gave them a few moments alone, anyway.

She glanced at the tray, looking both surprised and pleased. *Score one for his side.* "You said they made this?" she asked.

Trace nodded, then at the skeptical lift on her dark eyebrows, felt compelled to be a little more specific. "They got out the dishes and the tray. I did the actual cooking."

Some of the joy left her eyes. "I see," she said quietly, pulling her silk robe a little tighter around her waist. "Thank you. Now, if you don't mind—" She started to shut the door.

Trace palmed it open. "Actually, I think I'll join you."

She sighed but let him in. "Calling all the shots again?"

He watched the sway of her hips, the hint of bare calves, beneath her below-the-knee robe. Fresh from the shower, she had wrapped her hair in a towel, twisted, turban-style, atop her head. Her face was bare. Her lips soft. She had never looked or smelled sexier. It was all he could do to keep his hands to himself. But knowing they had important things to discuss, he sank onto a corner of the bed, watching as Susannah settled herself and her lunch tray on the window seat. "Somehow, I think there is more going on than what you have already said."

"Do you?" Susannah sipped her iced tea.

"Are you angry because I'm forcing you to marry me?"

No I'm hurt because you don't love me, Susannah thought, at least not enough to make our marriage work in any lasting way.

"What does it matter how I feel?" she countered. The bottom line is our relationship will never work long-term. Life is too precious and too short to spend it tied to someone you don't love." *And you don't love me.* "But I know you probably have legitimate concerns about our other...situation. So here's the deal," she continued with more equilibrium than she felt as she spread mustard on a sesame-seed bun with more than inordinate care. "I'll live at the hunting lodge here on the Silver Spur, just as Max wanted. You can see Scott as much as you want. You can give him a part-time job at the lumber company. You can take him fly-fishing and camping. Whatever you want in that regard. But no more using Scott as an excuse to punish me. No more forcing us to play out the loving couple." *No more making love to me like you mean it,* she finished silently.

"Is that what our lovemaking felt like to you? Punishment?"

Susannah recapped the mustard. "Or revenge. Or a means to an end."

Already deeply hurt by her misconceptions about him, Trace began to get angry, too. He had sacrificed a lot for her, *more than she knew.* "What about the boys?" he retorted argumentatively. "We may not have come right out and told them so, but they think we're in love again. They think what we have been feeling is the real thing."

And so, Trace admitted to himself, had he. Instead, his whole world was being turned upside down again by Susannah's abrupt change of heart. In the same way it had been when his parents had died and he and Cody and Patience had been sent to live with Max. In the way it had been when Susannah had left him the first time. He had worked hard to get his life in order again, to keep everything under control, and to have it all falling apart, so suddenly, and so completely, was almost more than he could bear.

Without any real energy, Susannah munched on the sandwich the boys had sent up to her. "I do feel guilty about confusing the boys the last couple of days."

"But?"

She lifted her eyes to his. "I'm determined to save us all from a lifetime of martyrdom and misery. I'm not going to turn into a nagging shrew. I am not going to spend the rest of my life, or even the next few years, fighting with you, paying for the past."

Trace shoved his hands into his pockets of his trousers and pushed to his feet. Abruptly, his mood turned brooding and dark. "When have we ever fought? Not when we were married, certainly. Things went so smoothly, in fact, that I thought everything was fine. Only to come home late one night, and get up the next morning to find you calmly telling me it was over as you were packing to leave.''

Susannah flinched at his blunt tone, but did not bend. ''It was best for us then, you weren't ready for a family,'' she asserted stubbornly, with another defiant lift of her chin.

That, Trace thought, was debatable. ''Was it the best thing to do?'' he challenged.

She gave him a pitying look. ''Don't you understand?'' she asked sadly, her slender shoulders bowed in defeat. ''The hurting each other has to be over, Trace. We can't bring this up every time we have a fight. I can't marry you knowing you resent me deep down. We've got to put the past where it belongs. Otherwise, I won't survive and neither will you.''

''That's easy for you to say, you weren't the one who was betrayed.''

The past forty-six and a half hours had given her hope things between them would be different. But then, what a fool she had been to think her deception could be so easily forgotten, Susannah thought despairingly.

''Look, I'm sorry,'' Trace said abruptly. The past is the past and we'll just forget it.''

''You obviously can't do that and I will not put our children through that,'' she told him sternly. ''You got your business deal this morning. The boys weren't hurt, they didn't hear our argument. That's great, but the happy outcome of all the calamity doesn't change a thing. You still resent what I've done. And you always will. And I almost can't blame you.''

TRACE STARED at Susannah. It hadn't felt that way to him. ''You think what we've shared the past two days and nights is a lie?'' He held out his hands and tried to take her in his arms. She brushed him away with short, choppy gestures.

''Realistically, what else was it, Trace? We pretended from the outset of our forty-eight hours to be falling in love so that the boys would accept our decision to stay married after we had collected our inheritances. As much as we might wish otherwise, *pretending something* is not the same as *feeling it.*''

Trace chalked up that move on his part to yet another mistake. ''No, it's not,'' he agreed, planting his legs apart as he prepared to attack and defend. And maybe this served him right, for trying to take shortcuts to a real and fulfilling relationship with her. Of course, at the time he had initiated said agreement, he hadn't known that was what he really wanted, either. Now that he had finally figured it out, it appeared to be too late, which was always the case with them, it seemed, too little, too late.

''Yes, we had passion,'' Susannah continued heatedly, some of the spark coming back into her eyes. ''Wonderful, exhilarating physical passion. I don't deny that for a minute. But as for anything else— Trace, can't you see?'' she asked, drawing her robe tighter around her slender form. ''We're all wrong for each other. We always have been. We always will be.''

We're all wrong for each other. We always have been. We always will be. Trace was devastated at his inability to intuitively do or say the right thing or make Susannah happy in any lasting way, for it was an echo of all his past failures when it came to personal relationships. It seemed all he had ever been able to do in any satisfying way was make love to her. And she was right, that wasn't enough, for either of them. It hadn't been before. Much as he was loath to admit it, it wouldn't be now. That being the case, she was right to call a halt.

"You're right," he said gruffly, almost glad she was sparing them the embarrassment of a second failed attempt at marriage and subsequent divorce. "If our relationship hasn't come together by now," he said grimly, "after all the time we spent together the past couple of days..." *after the night we spent together, baring our souls and making love.* "Then it never will."

1:09

"MOM DIDN'T LIKE the burger?" Mickey asked.

Trace could hardly blame her; considering the way things were going, he had no appetite, either. "She wasn't hungry," he told Mickey gently.

"I suppose she's too nervous to eat, huh, on account of the wedding is in an hour," Jason theorized.

"I don't think it was that, exactly." Trace poured himself some juice.

"She's upset about having to marry you, isn't she?" Scott supposed quietly as he polished off an apple.

Trace nodded and, glass in hand, sat down at the kitchen table with the boys. "My uncle Max meant well when he cooked up this plan to get us back together," he told them honestly, "but it isn't working out the way he planned."

"It could, if you weren't so quick to give up," Scott said casually.

"Who says I'm giving up?"

"Isn't it obvious?" Nate asked as he finished drinking the last of his milk. "I mean, you're getting married in a little over an hour, but you still look like you lost out on the best deal in your entire life."

"That's 'cause I have and we're not just talking about Susannah," Trace muttered.

Nate paused. The four boys exchanged glances. Finally, Scott asked, "Did something happen to the Farraday deal, too?"

Trace nodded, knowing they would all find out soon enough, anyway, and briefly explained. "It didn't happen."

Jason's eyes widened. "How come?" he gasped.

"Because I left before it could be completed," Trace explained.

"You're kidding, right?" Nate said.

Trace shook his head. "The bottom line is that some things—like the safety and welfare of a man's family and the happiness of the woman he loves—are more important than business." Unfortunately, he had come to that knowledge too late.

"Did you tell Mom about giving up the business deal?" Scott asked.

In every situation, there was a time to keep going, and a time to admit failure. Though it killed him to admit it, this was one of the times when persevering would be about as helpful as spinning the wheels of his Jeep in the mud. Trace finished his juice, and pushed away from the table. "Look, guys, I know you're trying to help," he said as he began to clear the table.

"More than that," Nate interrupted, leaping in to help, placing dishes in the dishwasher. "We're trying to get you to live up to your responsibilities."

"And follow through on this, all the way," Scott chimed in as he too, began to load the dishwasher.

Watching the way Scott pitched in and also cared for the other guys, Trace could see that Susannah had done a fine job parenting their son.

"What was it you said when we had that water fight, that combining two families under one roof required a team effort and we weren't doing our share," Jason reminded.

"Well, what about you now? Are you doing your share?" Mickey asked with wide-eyed innocence.

It was all Trace could do not to flush guiltily. "I've already talked to her."

"So?" Scott said.

"Talk to her again," Jason suggested.

"Yeah," Nate said. "Tell her you gave up that deal to come and save us."

Trace wished it were that simple. But it wasn't. Belatedly, he'd realized he had handled everything incorrectly from the beginning. Instead of demanding Susannah marry him, as some sort of vengeful punishment for the way she had once walked out on him and taken their son from him, he should have asked her why she had done what she did, and listened to what she had to say.

Because if he had done that right from the start, he would've understood how scared she'd been then, how scared she still was, and he would have courted her from the start, diligently and with tender loving care, and convinced her to marry him. Not because they had to get married, to share the rearing of their son, but because it was the right thing to do, because as different as they were, they still belonged together.

But he hadn't done any of that. And he could not go back and change that any more than he could change what had transpired between them seventeen years ago. There were some wounds that were simply too deep to heal.

He swallowed. Aware that the boys were waiting for him to continue, he said with genuine regret, "I'm sorry, guys, but it's too late. I've mishandled everything." He shook his head sadly. "Susannah will never forgive me for the many, many mistakes I made where she was concerned."

"You're wrong, Trace," Mickey said.

"Yeah," Scott chimed in. "Our mom is the quickest person to forgive that we know. Take our waterballoon fight, or even our disobeying you guys this morning and going down to have a look at the river. She was upset with us, and she had a right to be, but she got over it really fast. And you know why? 'Cause she loves us and she knows it's okay to make mistakes, to be human, that when you do something wrong, you pick yourself up, dust yourself off, right what you can and then go on."

Trace shrugged as they finished tidying the kitchen in record time. "Sounds like good advice," he said.

"You bet your bottom dollar it is," Nate agreed.

"So what makes this situation any different?" Jason asked.

Trace realized the four boys just might have a point.

00:59

"DAD IS REALLY SAD on account of us," Nate told Susannah the moment she walked out onto the deck to dry her hair in the sun.

Susannah perched on an adirondack chair and ran a comb through her hair. "What in the world makes you think that?"

"'Cause we messed everything up by running off to see the white water this morning," Jason replied. "And made him blow his business deal and everything."

Susannah blinked. "What are you talking about?"

All four boys exchanged trepidant glances. Finally, Nate said reluctantly, "He didn't get that property he wanted."

"Are you sure about that?"

The boys nodded solemnly. "He told us," Mickey said, looking worried.

Susannah paused in the act of combing the ends of her bobbed hair into a bell-shaped curve. "He didn't say anything to me about that." Surely he would have, especially since she knew how much that deal had meant to him.

Nate shrugged, looking almost as perplexed as she felt. "I guess he figured it wasn't important, with us missing and all."

"Yeah, we're sorry if we caused you any trouble," Jason added, digging the toe of his sneaker into the deck.

"I'm sure your father can finish the deal with Sam Farraday if he just explains what happened," Susannah soothed. She couldn't imagine a business deal Trace could not achieve.

"I don't think so," Scott said glumly.

"He didn't act that way," Mickey agreed.

"Besides, it isn't the business deal that fell through that has him really upset," Jason theorized.

"It's his fight with you, Susannah," Nate agreed.

Was it possible, Susannah wondered, beginning to hope despite herself, that Trace cared more about her than any business deal? She regarded all four boys gathered around her. "How do you know that?" she asked steadily.

"The way you guys were glaring at each other when you came to rescue us," Nate replied.

"It was pretty clear you'd been fighting about how come we were in that mess in the first place," Scott added quietly.

"Yeah," Jason agreed. "Dad thought it was your fault, you thought it was his, you know the drill."

Once again, she was surprised at the accurate assessment of the situation. Knowing the only way to reassure the boys was to be as honest as possible with them, Susannah admitted softly, "That's true, guys. We did think that way at first, but it was just because we were afraid something awful was going to happen to you kids. As soon as we knew you were all right, we stopped blaming each other for your temporary lapse in judgment."

"But you're still ticked off at each other," Jason persisted.

For reasons that went far beyond the morning's mishap, Susannah thought. But not wanting the boys upset by any of the difficulties between herself and Trace, she hedged, "I wouldn't say that exactly."

"It doesn't matter if you say it or not," Nate persisted.

"Yeah," Scott agreed. "We can feel it."

Aware her hair was nearly dry, Susannah stood. "I'm sorry we've upset you with our quarrel. That is something your dad and I never meant to do."

"It's not the quarrel that's upset us, it's your not making up after the quarrel that is getting to us," Nate said. "Mom and Dad used to disagree about stuff. But they always talked about it and cleared things up right away."

"How come you and Trace don't do that?" Mickey asked.

"Don't you want us to be together and live under one roof?" Jason persisted.

"'Cause we could've sworn by the way you two were always kissing and smiling at each other that you guys did want that," Scott concluded.

Susannah flushed. "We did."

"Then, what happened?" Jason asked.

"I don't know," Susannah said wistfully as she tightened her fingers around the teeth of the comb. "Things just sort of fell apart, the same way they did before."

"Did you try to fix them before?"

"Not really," Susannah replied slowly. *Not the way I wished we had.*

"Well, then, that being the case, don't you think you should this time?" Nate said. "I mean, if you and Dad care about each other at all..." His voice trailed off unhappily.

"I do love Trace, guys," Susannah told the boys. *I always have and always will.* And maybe if he had loved her, too, in the same way, they might have worked things out. But the way things had transpired, she didn't see that ever happening. And who could blame him, after she had betrayed him not once, but two, even three times. First by leaving, second by not telling him they were going to have a baby, third by walking out at the last minute on their remarriage plans, after he had already sacrificed a business deal that meant a lot to him as part of the price of being with her and their boys. "But this time, I've done something unforgivable and he isn't going to forgive me."

"Have you asked him?"

Susannah flushed with embarrassment. "It's not the kind of thing you ask, guys. Either it happens in here—" Susannah pointed to her heart "—or it doesn't."

Nate shrugged and pushed his glasses a little higher on the bridge of his nose. "Dad always says sometimes you gotta take a chance. And Dad can't do anything for you if you don't give him a chance. He's not a mind reader, you know. He says that to us all the time. You have to tell him what you need."

"Yeah, be blunt," Jason chimed in. "Dad likes it when people tell him what they need to succeed, because then he can just go right out and make it happen."

That did sound like Trace.

"Well?" all four boys asked breathlessly at once.

Susannah knew there was one thing she wanted from Trace, a second chance to do over this new beginning of theirs, and to do it right this time. But was it too late? Uncle Max had told them in his will there was no use crying over spilt milk. He had advised them to listen to their hearts, because if they did, they would know what to do. She knew what her heart was telling her to do.

Susannah glanced at her watch. She and Trace still had time for a private conversation. And more. That was, if he was willing to hear her out. "Is your father dressed?" she asked anxiously.

"Oh, we almost forgot." Jason slapped his forehead.

"There's a button on his shirt that got ripped off," Nate said.

"Yeah," Mickey chimed in.

"He asked you to come, and bring your sewing kit," Scott relayed the message lazily.

Susannah blinked. Under the circumstances, she couldn't imagine Trace asking her for any favors. Nor could she imagine the ever-efficient Cisco Kidd delivering wedding clothes to the lake house that were not in tip-top condition: Susannah's wedding gown sure was. On the other hand, maybe it was just an excuse on Trace's part, to talk to her, and try again. At least she could hope.

"But you better hurry." Nate consulted his watch.

"Yeah," Mickey agreed as Scott nodded solemnly at his side.

"We don't want to miss the wedding," Jason said.

Chapter Twelve

00:51

"Okay, where's the button?" Susannah asked as she swept into the master bedroom, the full skirt of her white satin wedding dress rustling around her, her travel sewing kit in hand.

Trace emerged from the adjacent bathroom, starched white tuxedo shirt in one hand, a small white button in another. The hair on his chest glowed golden against the suntanned hue of his skin. As he regarded her curiously, the bunched muscles in his chest and shoulders tensed. "How'd you know about that?" he asked, his gaze drifting lazily over the fitted lacy bodice, short off-the-shoulder cap sleeves and portrait neckline of her dress.

Susannah drew in a whiff of his cologne as she neared. He was never sexier than when half-dressed. "The same way I know everything around here—" her lips curved in an amused smile "—our young grapevine of perpetual information. They said you needed some sewing help."

Trace handed over both shirt and button. He sat down on the edge of his bed, watched as Susannah settled next to him. "I admit I wasn't having much luck paper-clipping it closed."

They turned at the sound of a door closing, and then a soft click and a thud. Trace quirked an eyebrow, as did she. Without warning, Susannah's heart was racing.

"You part of that?" he drawled.

"No," Susannah replied cautiously, wondering if he was feeling even half as reckless as she felt. "You?"

Trace shook his head.

Her heart pounding at this unexpected development, Susannah rose and gracefully retraced her steps. She cocked her ear and bent toward the door. The sounds of whispering and giggling could be heard on the other side. Generally speaking, this was not a good sign. "Okay, guys, what's going on?" she demanded, trying hard not to be amused by the obvious matchmaking of their children.

Utter silence.

Susannah tugged on the knob. As expected, it didn't budge. She turned around to look at Trace, a new wave of color sweeping into her cheeks. She cleared her throat delicately. "It would appear we are locked in."

Trace scowled and started to rise.

"Guys, this isn't funny," Susannah warned lyrically through the closed door as Trace stealthily made his way to her side.

"Tell us about it!" Jason said.

"Yeah!" Mickey enthused.

"We're taking matters into our own hands!" Nate vowed.

"You two are grounded until you make up!" Scott added.

More nervous laughter followed.

Listening, Trace looked more than a little irritated. "Guys, let us out," Trace ordered.

"No way, Dad. We want you two together and we've all decided to do whatever it takes to make sure that happens," Jason said.

There was a pause, and then Nate finished, "I know Uncle Max would've approved."

"We'll be waiting in our rooms," Mickey said.

"The way we see it, you've got approximately ten minutes to make up, if we still want to get to the wedding on time," Scott finished.

Footsteps receded down the hall.

Trace leaned against the door, suddenly seeming in no particular hurry to get out of there. His deep blue eyes lasered in on hers. "Sounds like they've planned this out well."

"They *are* our kids," Susannah smiled. "What could we expect?"

They stared at each other in silence. The silence gave way to sheepish smiles. Susannah knew Trace understood kids as well as she did. And their kids wanted them together, too. The question was, what did Trace want? Suddenly, she was almost afraid to find out.

Chin high, she headed back to the sewing kit she'd left on the bed. "As long as I'm here, and we have a few minutes, I might as well sew on that button for you," she murmured.

Trace followed her lazily and sat down opposite her. He watched her thread a needle and tie a knot on the end. "You don't mind?"

Susannah centered the button on the shirt, and aware her hands were trembling just a tad, made the first stitch. "All you had to do was ask."

Trace stood and paced to the window and back. "If only our relationship was this uncomplicated in all areas."

"It could be," Susannah replied, quickly moving the needle in and out of the buttonholes.

Trace's glance fell to her hands before returning to her face. He eyed her determinedly. "I'm listening," he said with a quiet implacability that sent shivers of awareness racing down her spine.

It was time to risk or spend the rest of her life regretting. "Remember when you asked me to help you draw up a marriage contract for us, so you would know what my expectations were?" she told him emotionally as she finished sewing the button and snipped the thread.

Trace grimaced apologetically. He held out his arms as she stood, stepped behind him and helped him into his shirt. "It was a dumb idea," he said, turning around to face her. Nimbly, he began to button his shirt. "We don't need to spell out what goes on in our relationship every minute of every day, in order to make our marriage work."

Our marriage. Present tense. Did that mean he hadn't entirely given up on them, either? Susannah wondered with trepidation.

"On the other hand," she said, almost too casually, watching as he tucked the tails of his shirt into his black tuxedo pants, zipped them up and redid his belt buckle. "It helps to know your partner's expectations, in business or personal life."

She stepped nearer to help him with his tie. "It's not so out-of-line to want to know what those expectations are." She straightened the black satin bow. Dropping her hands to his shoulders, she drew a deep breath. "I was wrong to leave you before, without giving us a chance to work things out. And I'm sorry for that," she told him on a trembling sigh.

"I'm sorry, too." His voice was husky with regret as he wrapped his arms around her waist and gathered her close. "For letting you down. For letting us all down."

Tears of happiness shimmered in Susannah's eyes as she twined her arms around his neck. "I want a second chance, Trace. I want to do it right this time."

His handsome face split into a relieved grin. He brushed his lips over her temple. "So do I." He paused to kiss her on the lips, sweetly, lingeringly. He tugged her closer so they were aligned more intimately yet. He looked down at her hotly and confessed, "I want to follow the dictates of my heart, just as Max advised. I want to be with you for the rest of my life—" he kissed her cheek, her temple, the curve of her ear "—and love you the way you were meant to be loved." His hands molded her spine. "The way I have always loved you."

Their lips met again. Joy unlike anything Susannah had ever known swept through her. He did love her, after all! "Oh, Trace, I love you, too," she murmured emotionally, clinging to him, and their future, with all her might. "I never stopped."

"Then it's settled?" Trace tightened his hold on her. "We won't just go through with the wedding for formality's sake. We'll get married today as planned. And the boys will be ours. And we'll find a way to explain to Scott that I'm his father—together."

"Oh, Trace... It will be all right."

Trace nodded his agreement. "But we'll start with our honeymoon to—"

"The day after tomorrow."

Trace paused. "The day after?" he asked, confused.

Susannah nodded. It was time to reveal her gift to him. "I called the travel agency that made the arrangements for Max. They're going to move them back a day, so you will have time to meet with Sam Farraday and her attorney again tomorrow. I called her and explained why you had to get up and leave in the middle of the meeting. Though single and childless, she has a strong dose of female intuition herself, and she was surprisingly understanding once I explained. The deal is on again, for tomorrow morning."

Trace looked stunned but happy as he sat down in a chair and tugged her down onto his lap, "I thought you resented my devotion to business."

Susannah draped her arm around his shoulders and cuddled against him. The love in his eyes was as sure and strong as the love in her heart and she knew this time that it would last a lifetime. "That was when I thought your business fell ahead of family in your priorities," she admitted as he continued to hold her protectively close. "Finding out it didn't... that you had sacrificed the Farraday deal to follow what at the time was merely my intuition that the boys were in danger... made me realize you had changed, and for the better. And if you could sacrifice something so important to you, for the sake of our family," she continued, her lower lip quivering, "it was time I made some changes in my behavior, too, and stopped viewing your hard work as a rival for my affections. 'Cause I know now, it's not."

"You're right, it isn't, not by a long shot." He kissed her softly, lingeringly.

"Besides, sacrificing one day of our honeymoon was a small price to pay for a lifetime of married bliss," Susannah said happily.

"Now, that sounds good to me." He paused to give her another long, sensual kiss. Reluctantly, noting the time, recalling their pending nuptials, they drew apart. His strong fingers closing tightly over hers, he led her to the window, removed the screen and studied the possibilities with an experienced eye. "Now all we have to do is get out of here," he said.

00:38

"I TOLD YOU it would work," Nate whispered from his vantage point down the hall.

"How do you know?" Scott asked, frowning, as he struggled to help his younger brother with his black-satin bow tie.

"Do you hear any fighting?" Jason queried, swiftly tying his tennis shoes.

"No," Mickey said.

All four boys exchanged glances. "What do you think that means?" Jason asked as he flattened a hand over his cowlick.

Scott shrugged and started to work on his own bow tie. "They could be kissing."

"Guess again!" a low voice rumbled behind them.

The four boys started and whirled toward Trace. "How did you get out here in the hall?" they demanded in unison.

"That," Trace told them as he swept by them and moved the chair wedged beneath the door handle, "is for me to know and you boys never to try." He removed the mangled paper clip that had interfered with the lock, opened the door and let Susannah out.

Looking like a vision in her white wedding dress, she swept to his side, smiling all the while. There was no mistaking the happiness in her eyes.

Taking her hand in his, he announced, "I'm glad to see you're all in your tuxes, guys, 'cause Susannah and I have some very good news to share."

00:25

WHEN THE WHOOPS and hollers had subsided, and congratulatory hugs had been exchanged all around, Trace glanced at his watch, then at Susannah. "Think we can make it?"

Susannah adjusted her veil and tucked her hand in his. They had a little more than twenty minutes to get to the wedding. "If we leave right now, we can," she assured her guys.

They all piled into her Suburban. Leaving the lake house was the easy part. It was when they hit the main ranch road that they fell into trouble. Water was pooled in some of the low-lying dips in the road. Trace slowed the Suburban and the first shallow puddles were navigated without problem. The fourth was deeper than it looked. They swept through it, then promptly bogged down in mud on the other side.

As the car stopped going forward, the wheels spun. The vehicle sank even more. Swearing, Trace shifted into park and cut the engine. "You all stay here," he ordered firmly. "I'm going to get out and take a look."

They waited with bated breath for Trace to circle the car and take a look. Susannah leaned out the window. "How bad is it?" she asked.

Trace was already stripping off his jacket and rolling up his sleeves. "Bad."

00:15

TRACE OPENED the cargo doors to the back of the Suburban. He took a small shovel out of the tire well. "We've got to dig out and get some traction under these wheels."

"What are we going to use?"

"I don't know." Trace paused to look at the woods on either side of them. There were downed branches here, too. Most were three or four feet in length. "I guess we could try the brush."

"Hang on, Dad. We'll get it." Before he could stop them, Nate and Jason jumped out of the truck and into the mud. Scott and Mickey were fast on their heels. In tandem, they struggled toward the woods.

"How far are we from the wedding site?" Susannah asked.

"Ten minutes." Trace bent and scooped out another shovelful of mud. "Assuming," he added grimly, clearing out the mud around first one wheel, then the next, "there are no more snafus."

The boys came back, dragging several leafy-green branches apiece. "How are these, Dad?"

"Great." Trace pointed toward the front wheel he'd dug out. "Push what you can underneath the wheel."

"We're running out of time. I'll help you dig, too," Scott said, flinging off his tuxedo jacket. He took a separate branch and began digging out beneath a rear wheel.

"I'll work on this one." Nate took his place at the other rear wheel. Meanwhile, Jason and Mickey helped Trace stick branches beneath the front wheels. Two minutes later, they circled to the back. All four boys crammed as much foliage as they could beneath the wheels.

Trace motioned everyone away from the truck. The muddied crew was quick to obey.

"Want me to try it?" Susannah asked.

Trace nodded.

She slid behind the wheel. Started the engine, shifted into gear and gave it the gas.

She rocked forward slightly, then back. Feeling the truck begin to sink again, she stopped and put it back into park.

"The branches won't do it," Trace said. "We need something else."

"How about our coats?" Scott asked.

Nate nodded his agreement. "That's bound to give us better traction."

Trace hated to do it, but what choice did they have? "Okay." He shrugged, a little amazed at how quickly they had become a family in just two days. "Let's give it a try." The boys rushed forward. With Trace directing, they shoved their jackets under all four wheels.

They all stepped back, clear of the truck. He turned to Susannah.

"Ready?" she said.

He nodded. "Give it another try."

Susannah started the engine, shifted into drive and hit the gas. The Suburban rocked forward, back, then lurched forward.

She drove until she hit gravel again. Then braked. Whooping and cheering with joy, Trace and the boys dashed to catch. "How much time?" Nate asked as Susannah scooted over so Trace could get behind the wheel.

00:02

"WE'RE NOT GOING to make it," Jason said as he, too, glanced at his watch.

"We can try! Drive fast, Dad," Nate urged.

"Yeah, real fast," Mickey coaxed.

"No," Trace said firmly. With Scott reaching driving age soon, it was imperative he set a good example. "We'll get there safely or not at all."

"But your inheritance," the boys protested in unison.

"Is the least of our worries," Trace said as he reached over and squeezed Susannah's hand. He glanced at the boys in the rearview mirror. "We've already got everything we need, one another." He could live without his inheritance. He couldn't live without Susannah and the boys; she was the key to his happiness; the key to his heart. Now and forever.

-00:13

"Look, Dad, there really is a wedding going on," Jason stated in a hushed reverent tone. "Two weddings. See. There's Uncle Cody and his bride."

"Man, she's a looker!" Scott enthused.

"And Aunt Patience and is that...Dr. Colter, the new veterinarian?" Nate asked.

"It would appear so," Trace said.

Without warning, the audience erupted in applause. The orchestra started up again and Cody and his bride, Callie Sheridan, and Patience and Josh Colter, started back down the satin aisles.

"It's over." Trace looked at Susannah. "We may have missed out on our inheritances, but it's still not too late to get married again today, if you don't mind a little mud, that is."

Susannah grinned. "I say, let's find the minister and do it!"

The boys cheered again, just as Trace's family came rushing at him.

"Where were you?" Patience demanded.

"We waited as long as we could," Cody said.

"They had to marry, as the will stated," Cisco explained.

Trace held up a hand to stop the flow of explanations. "It's okay. We know we've lost our inheritances, by not marrying within forty-eight hours," he said happily. And thanks to the love he had found with Susannah, it really didn't matter.

"Not necessarily."

They turned at the sound of the deep, booming voice. A collective gasp went through the crowd.

"Max?" Patience, Trace and Cody said in unison, the color leaving their faces.

"One and the same." Big as life, his silver spurs jingling, Max strode toward them. He was clad in his usual fringed buckskins. He swept off his Stetson, revealing his mane of snowy-white hair and a grin as big as all Montana. "As you can see, the reports of my death have been greatly exaggerated," he drawled.

"But," Cody sputtered. Patience looked as if she might faint. Only Trace, greatly irritated, turned to Max's attorney.

Cisco palmed his chest. "Don't look at me," he said. "I was just following orders."

Max nodded vigorously, attesting that was true, then continued explaining, "I figured why wait until I actually kicked the bucket to give you young'uns your inheritances? Why not do it while I'm still alive to enjoy it," Max said. He spread his arms wide. "So I did."

"Or in my case, you tried." Trace shook his head.

It was Max's turn to hold up a cautioning palm. "Not to worry, Trace and Susannah," he informed them gently. "You're still going to get what's coming to you, once you say your I dos. Not that it's necessary in the legal sense."

Trace regarded his uncle. He could tell by the glimmer in Max's wily blue eyes that his eccentric uncle was not done with his surprises. "What do you mean, it's not necessary?" he asked.

"You know that quickie divorce you asked me to get for you, seventeen years ago?" Max slapped his knee as his family gathered around. "Well, it seems there was a hitch with it. The papers were never filed. So, technically, you and Susannah are still married...have been all this time," he said as a gasp ran through the crowd.

"I found out about it myself about the same time that Callie signed up with the Western Ranch Wives video-matchmaking service, and Patience told me she was thinking of going to a clinic to have her baby," Max explained. With a shrug, he continued, "With so much happening at once, I figured Providence had to be sending me a sign. And since I was part and parcel of all three of your romances going sour, I figured I should be part and parcel of all three getting fixed. So, I came up with the idea to reunite you all. Cisco helped me write the will. And here we all are."

Patience thrust herself into Max's arms. She gave him a fierce hug. Cody and Trace swiftly followed suit. Tears and laughter were all around. "But what are you going to do?" Patience asked.

"Good question," Max said. He looked at his sidekick and attorney, Cisco Kidd, and then his old friend and town-diner owner, Pearl. "But don't you all worry none," Max told them seriously. "I've got plenty of new frontiers to conquer. I'm hoping Pearl will go with me. And Cisco, as a way of thanking you for all you've done for me and my kin, just let me tell you that your future is set, too. As it should be, since you've become like a son to me."

"And a brother to us," Patience said as Trace and Cody agreed.

For once, the handsome Montana attorney was at a loss for words. Cisco swept off his hat and ran a hand through his hair. "I have to admit, Max, I had my doubts when you came up with this idea, but it seems everything worked out even better than any of us could have hoped."

"I'll damn sure second that." Max grinned. "Here's to the future." Max lifted his glass of champagne in a toast.

Cisco locked eyes with Gillian Taylor as everyone followed suit. Trace thought, but couldn't be sure, he saw a flash of attraction there. One that might possibly bring the quiet Cisco out of his shell. He couldn't think of anything that would please him more.

"May it bring us all much love and happiness," Trace proposed, wrapping his arm around his beloved and drawing her close.

"Right here on the Silver Spur," Susannah agreed. They clinked glasses and drank their toast.

"Hey, I thought you two were getting married," Mickey reminded them, tugging on Susannah's skirt and Trace's sleeve.

Trace held out his hand to Susannah. "We are," he said firmly as the beaming minister stepped forward out of the crowd. "And we'll need four witnesses," Trace said. "Scott, Nate, Jason, Mickey—"

"Can we count on you to help us out?" Susannah asked.

"You bet," the boys said in unison, gathering round, and the ceremony that would bind them together the rest of their lives began.

BRIDE'S BAY RESORT

UNLOCK THE DOOR TO GREAT ROMANCE AT BRIDE'S BAY RESORT

Join Harlequin's new across-the-lines series, set in an exclusive hotel on an island off the coast of South Carolina.

Seven of your favorite authors will bring you exciting stories about fascinating heroes and heroines discovering love at Bride's Bay Resort.

Look for these fabulous stories coming to a store near you beginning in January 1996.

Harlequin American Romance #613 in January
Matchmaking Baby by Cathy Gillen Thacker

Harlequin Presents #1794 in February
Indiscretions by Robyn Donald

Harlequin Intrigue #362 in March
Love and Lies by Dawn Stewardson

Harlequin Romance #3404 in April
Make Believe Engagement by Day Leclaire

Harlequin Temptation #588 in May
Stranger in the Night by Roseanne Williams

Harlequin Superromance #695 in June
Married to a Stranger by Connie Bennett

Harlequin Historicals #324 in July
Dulcie's Gift by Ruth Langan

Visit Bride's Bay Resort each month wherever Harlequin books are sold.

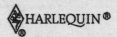

HARLEQUIN ®

BBAYG

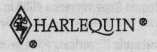

HARLEQUIN®

A M E R I C A N ◆ R O M A N C E ®

Their idea of a long night is a sexy woman and a warm
bed—not a squalling infant!

To them, a "bottle" means champagne—not formula!

But these guys are about to get a rude awakening!
They're about to become

Join us next month for:

#638 LIKE FATHER, LIKE SON
by Mollie Molay

Look us up on-line at: http://www.romance.net

AD-2

HARLEQUIN®

AMERICAN ◆ ROMANCE®

*He's at home in denim; she's bathed in diamonds...
Her tastes run to peanut butter; his to pâté...
They're bound to be together*

for
Richer,
for
Poorer

We're delighted to bring you more of the kinds of stories
you love in FOR RICHER, FOR POORER—where lovers
are drawn by passion...but separated by price!

Next month, look for:

#640 BLUE-JEANED PRINCE

By Vivian Leiber

Don't miss any of the
FOR RICHER, FOR POORER
books—only from American Romance!

FRFP-2

A NEW STAR COMES OUT TO SHINE....

American Romance continues to search the heavens for the best new talent... the best new stories.

Join us next month when a new star appears in the American Romance constellation:

Liz Ireland
#639 HEAVEN-SENT HUSBAND
July 1996

Ellen couldn't believe her former husband placed a personal ad for her—her *dead* former husband! Well, at least that explained the strange men showering her with calls and gifts, including Simon Miller. Ellen was attracted to Simon—but how was a girl supposed to start a relationship when her dead husband kept lurking over her shoulder?

RISING STAR

Be sure to Catch a "Rising Star"!

STAR696

If you are looking for more titles by

CATHY GILLEN THACKER

Don't miss these fabulous stories by one of
Harlequin's most renowned authors:

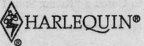

HARLEQUIN®

HARLEQUIN®
AMERICAN ◆ ROMANCE®

American Romance is about to ask that most important question:

Where were you when the lights went out?

When a torrid heat wave sparks a five-state blackout on the Fourth of July, three women get caught in unusual places with three men whose sexiness alone could light up a room! What these women do in the dark, they sure wouldn't do with the lights on!

Don't miss any of the excitement in:

#637 NINE MONTHS LATER...
By Mary Anne Wilson
July 1996

#641 DO YOU TAKE THIS MAN...
By Linda Randall Wisdom
August 1996

#645 DEAR LONELY IN L.A....
By Jacqueline Diamond
September 1996

Don't be in the dark—read
WHERE WERE YOU WHEN THE LIGHTS WENT OUT?—
only from American Romance!

Look us up on-line at: http://www.romance.net

BLACKOUT

OUTB